Stephen Cullen

The Haunted Priory

A Romance Founded Principally on Historical Facts

Stephen Cullen

The Haunted Priory
A Romance Founded Principally on Historical Facts

ISBN/EAN: 9783744674294

Printed in Europe, USA, Canada, Australia, Japan

Cover: Foto ©Andreas Hilbeck / pixelio.de

More available books at **www.hansebooks.com**

THE

HAUNTED PRIORY;

OR,

THE FORTUNES OF

THE HOUSE OF RAYO,

A ROMANCE

FOUNDED PRINCIPALLY ON HISTORICAL FACTS.

BY STEPHEN CULLEN,

THE THIRD EDITION.

————Hic murus aheneus esto,
Nil conscire sibi, nulla pallescere culpa

LONDON:

PRINTED FOR J. BELL,
NO. 148, OXFORD-STREET, OPPOSITE BOND-STREET,
MDCCXCVI.

THE
HAUNTED PRIORY.

CHAP. I.

IT was on a cold and ſtormy December even‑ing in the beginning of the fourteenth century, and not long after that fortunate period when Peter ſurnamed the Cruel was cut off from a life which he had ſtained with bloodſhed, rapine, and oppreſſion, that a ſtranger entered a village ſituated on the banks of the Tagus, near the eaſtern extremity of the kingdom of Caſtile in Spain. He was old, and, though withered, of gigantic ſtature—his large ſnow-white beard ſtreamed in the ſleeting wind—a great coat of black baize was buckled with a leathern belt

about

about his loins—he had on his feet fandals inftead of fhoes, and on his back he carried a large harp; while a long ftaff, ornamented on the top with a crofs, fuftained his wearied fteps. He ftopped at the door of the firft neat-looking cottage that prefented itfelf, and, afking whether he could be accommodated with lodging for the night, was anfwered in the affirmative, and requefted to walk in. Being feated, at the defire of the people of the houfe, he told them that he wanted not only lodging for the night, but food alfo; and apprifed them at the fame time that he had nothing to offer them in return, but his prayers and a tune of his harp.

Your prayers we earneftly defire, father, replied a young man—but other return we wifh not, nor fhould accept. Even your harp, whatever delight it might afford us, fhall remain untouched, if offered in way of compenfation for any little accommodation our poor hut can beftow—And indeed, continued he, I confider it to be a fortunate circumftance that you fhould have called at this particular feafon of the year, when, in conformity to the eftablifhed cuftoms of our country, we are provided with better means of entertaining you than we fhould be at any other time.

A feeble fuffufion of red, that befpoke fomething more than gratitude, overfpread the aged

face

face of the Pilgrim—he laid his hands upon his breaft—bent his head in acknowledgment—paufed —then fighed and faid, while his words feemed ftruggling for a paffage, He that infpireth thy heart, good youth! with the true fpirit of bene-ficence will give thee the reward of it.

A table was then fpread with the beft provifions which the cottage afforded—and the whole family, confifting of the young man already mentioned, his wife, an old man his father, and two chil-dren, fat down with the ftranger to a frugal but wholefome fupper : a pitcher of tolerable wine concluded the feaft, the young man earneftly preffing his aged gueft to drink.

The enlivening influence of hofpitality, and the unaffected cheerfulnefs and good nature of the cottagers, infenfibly relaxed the aufterity of the old Pilgrim, and warmed him into converfation—He liftened with pleafure to the fimple detail of ruftic enjoyment, and the artlefs acknowledgments of domeftic blifs——At length, Happy, fays he, my fon! moft fupremely happy is thy lot, if there be happinefs found on earth, and you have the wifdom to underftand it—God has given thee greater riches than are to be found in the palaces of princes, or the ftately domes of the affluent. I re-member the time indeed, when the caftle of a no-bleman, or the arm of a knight, were the never-fail-

ing

ing refuge of diftrefs in whatfoever garb diftrefs appeared, and when the proud turrets of the nobility burft upon the fight of the oppreffed or unfortunate, like the firft beams of the orient fun on the eye of the night-ftrayed traveller; cheering, enlivening, and diffufing hope and joy—Then reigned over this happy country Alphonfo the wife, the valiant, and the good—But now at every gate favage inhofpitality with ftern denial rudely oppofes the entrance of the poor, and chills the woe-worn heart of mifery; but crouches and bafely bends the fervile knee of refpect to the pampered knave of fortune—O gracious God!—from fuch let my fteps be turned for ever.

Ah, father! interrupted the young man, pardon the prefumption of youthful zeal, which thus ventures to break on your difcourfe: but little fhould I merit your good opinion, if I fuffered you uninformed to fay that now, which to-morrow's fetting fun fhould fee thee retract—To-morrow, God willing, thou fhalt fee a man.

What man? interrupted the ftranger warmly.

Oh! fuch a man!—the hufband of the widow—the father of the orphan—the never-failing refource of the diftreffed—humble though wealthy—though valiant, gentle as the new-dropt lamb.

Young man, your youthful heart, impreffed with fome partial act of generofity, fome unimportant

portant benefit, rendered perhaps in a moment of capricious virtue, overflows with a gratitude which blinds you ; a gratitude which fpeaks more for you than for the object of it :—generous yourfelf, you over-rate the favours conferred upon you by others—This is an error, but I confefs an amiable one, and no uncertain pledge of a worthy heart—But who is this man, this very fingular character of whom you fpeak ?

Here every mouth involuntarily opened, and at the fame inftant pronounced Don Ifidor.

Don Ifidor !—who ? what Don Ifidor ? impatiently exclaimed the Pilgrim.

Don Ifidor de Haro, returned the hoft.

Don Ifidor de Haro !—Good Heavens !—— Young man, recollect yourfelf—fay—what Don Ifidor de Haro—is he of this country—or how long has he lived in it ?

As to his native country, I cannot fay any thing with certainty, returned the young man; but I believe he is a Caftilian by birth—He has been here but a fhort time, yet in that fhort time has gained the affections of all ranks of people.

Here the old man of the cottage took up the account with—It is only two years fince Don Ifidor came here to take pofleffion of the caftle and eftate of Duero, which he honourably obtained from the affection of our good king as a reward for his

fervices :

fervices :—where he came from I know not, but I have heard that he was all his life before in the wars.

The ftranger rofe fuddenly from his feat, took two or three hafty ftrides acrofs the room, fighed bitterly; then again fitting down feemed entranced in meditation, while the whole family, ftruck with awful aftonifhment at his evident perturbation, remained filent—At length, fomewhat recovering himfelf—Pardon, good people, faid he, the emotions occafioned by the fudden recollection of fome paffages of a life ftrangely checquered with the viciffitudes of fortune.—But this Don Ifidor de Haro, then, is a good man, you fay, though rich !—Is he married ?

He was married, but his lady had been dead fome time before his coming here ; his domeftics fay that forrow for her death has driven him to this retired life. His grief feems unaltered and undiminifhed by time, though it is faid that he was at the firft quite ferene and calm under it.

Has he any children ?——

Yes, father ! he has two : the young gentleman Don Alphonfo, his eldeft, is now about fourteen years of age.

Alphonfo ! has he indeed a fon named Alphonfo ?

He has—the nobleft youth that lives—I have the
honour

honour to be employed by Don Ifidor as one of, his inftructors.

Then you are a fcholar ?

Thanks to Providence, I am not entirely ignorant of letters, but by no means fuch a fcholar as to inftruct that young gentleman in letters—Father Thomas who lives at the caftle does that, but I teach and practife him in fome of the athletic exercifes ; for you muft know that there is not one neceffary to a foldier, or becoming a gentleman, in which he is not diligently inftructed ; nor is there a youth of fome years older than him in the country, that can equal him at any of them :—befides, he is reckoned a moft accomplifhed fcholar for his age ; and as to his perfon, you will judge of that when you fee it : I will not pretend to defcribe it.

Donna Ifabella the daughter, continued he, is about eight years old, they fay, but has been ever fince her mother's death with a fifter of Don Ifidor, who is married to a nobleman in the court of Portugal ; and it is faid by the domeftics that fhe is a child of unequalled beauty ; and that as Don Alphonfo fhews in every motion the fpirit and vigour of Don Ifidor, fo Donna Ifabella every day difclofes more and more the delicate luftre of beauty, and excellent temper of her deceafed mother.

Don Ifidor then muft be happy, cried the Pilgrim.

Pilgrim. Bleſt with wealth, power, children ſuch as you deſcribe, and, above all, with the well-merited affections of his vaſſals and dependents, he muſt approach as near to happineſs as the ſtate of mortality will allow.

Some ſay not, replied the peaſant. Thoſe who have the conſtant opportunity of obſerving him remark, that he labours under ſome hidden melancholy : indeed, all allow that he has never been the ſame ſince the death of his lady; and were it not for the amuſements he finds in the inſtruction of his ſon, the employment of his mind in contriving and executing acts of beneficence, and in the converſation of the good Father Thomas, it is thought that he muſt have ſunk beneath the weight of his afflictions.—Indeed, Father Thomas is a moſt excellent man ; for, beſides his extraordinary piety, he is extremely charitable, and as a preacher and paſtor is unequalled :— but to-morrow, father, you will ſee them all— Don Iſidor will expect you. No one, whatever his condition may be, paſſes withour calling at the caſtle ; and it is a part of the young gentleman Alphonſo's buſineſs to watch leſt they ſhould accidentally paſs by, and to bring them home with him, from whence they generally carry away a good ſupply of clothes and food. Nay, I doubt not but that while we indulge ourſelves here with the enjoyment

joyment of your company, we may run the hazard of difobliging Don Ifidor by not having conducted you to him at firft.

Little more paffed that night—The fatigues of the day called upon the old ftranger to retire to his room, and the cottagers fought, by timely repofe, to prepare for the labours of the enfuing day.

C H A P.

C H A P. II.

NEXT morning the Pilgrim, after having beſtowed on his hoſts a hearty benediction, and his thanks for their hoſpitable ſhelter, took his leave, and proceeded on his way towards the caſtle of Duero. It was little leſs than a quarter of a league from the cottage to the avenue ; and as he walked very ſlowly, deeply immerſed in thought, the day was advanced when he got to the gate of it. Here ſeeing that the manſion was at a diſtance little ſhort of that which he had already come, he ſat himſelf down upon a large ſtone bench in order to reſt himſelf, and diſcuſs at leiſure the variety of ſubjects which occupied his thoughts from the diſcourſe of the preceding night.—He had not been very long ſeated when he perceived a number of boys running towards him with the ſpeed of a flock of frighted deer ; one outſtripped the reſt, and, leaving them far behind, reached the ſtranger before he had time to form a conjecture upon the novelty of his appearance. If the old man was ſurpriſed at the ſwiftneſs of his pace, he was

aſtoniſhed

astonished at his personal appearance, and still more at his address. The full, muscular conformation of his limbs, and the large size of his bones, displayed a stature gigantic for his age, and promised a proportionate share of strength : his face, in which manly fire, dignity and sensibility were blended, glowed with the colours of health and exercise; while an air at once majestic and insinuating diffused a charm over the whole, that operated like a spell upon the beholder. Addressing the old man with a mixture of respect, admiration and pity, he said, I hope, Señor, you have not been long sitting in this place so unworthy your reverend appearance and years; should it be so, I shall have to accuse myself of an unpardonable neglect, for which I should certainly receive a severe reproof from Don Isidor. How far have you travelled this morning? have you breakfasted, or taken any refreshments? and seeing a moisture collecting in the old man's eyes, Do, dear Sir, get up, and I will lead you to a place where you shall refresh yourself with food and repose, and where you will meet with a hearty reception. Here he reached forth his hand to the Pilgrim, who grasping it in a mixed ecstasy of transport and amazement, snatched it hastily to his lips, and bedewed it with tears of affection. O wondrous youth! exclaimed he, whosoever thou art, whom God has
formed

formed on a model all his own, lead on—I will follow, you any where—every where.—He could no more—utterance was choked in the tumult of his feelings, and he walked flowly along, his young guide holding him by one of his fingers, which he had caught in the excefs of his rapture, and ftill retained with a firm grafp, while the other boys, who had come up one after the other, furrounded them, gazing alternately at the beard, the drefs, and the harp which hung at the back of the Pilgrim.

As they proceeded along—Is Don Ifidor at home, my dear? interrogated the old man.—No, Señor, he has been abroad for fome days; but all the fervant have directions to obey punctually my orders in my father's abfence, and you fhall be well treated though he be not at home. To be fure, he will be greatly delighted on his return, which is now hourly expected, to find you here; for nothing gives him fo much pleafure as the company of ftrangers: at the fartheft, he will certainly be back to-morrow: mean time, whenever my talk wearies you, Father Thomas will keep you in converfation more entertaining, as well as more fuitable to the gravity of your years.

At length they arrived at the gate of the caftle. On its being opened, the ftranger was furprifed to find himfelf faluted with as much refpect as if

he

he had been a prince, by the keeper, who empha-
tically pronounced, Welcome, ftranger, who-
foever thou art, welcome to the caftle of Duero!
The old man felt fenfations to which he had long
been a ftranger. As they paffed through the
court-yard, they were accofted by a fervant, who
faid, Don Alphonfo, the horfes are ready. It is very
well, Pierot, replied the youth; I will but introduce this ftranger to Father Thomas, and attend
directly. Upon which the Pilgrim turning to his
young friend faid, Let me not, I befeech you,
young gentleman, detain you from your pleafures.
Though the days of youth are paft with me, I
well remember the painfulnefs of reftraint; and
I already feel too great an intereft in your heart,
to run the hazard of lofing any fhare of it by tax-
ing your kindnefs too feverely.

Indeed, returned the youth, the delight I
feel in attending you would more than compen-
fate for the lofs of any pleafure. The fervant who
juft now fpoke, came to call me to my riding-
mafter: riding is a part of my daily exercife; but
attending you is a duty much more material in
itfelf, and much more productive of pleafure to
me.

Having brought his gueft into the houfe, Alphonfo led him into the great hall, placed him in
the chair, and gave orders that immediate preparation

ration fhould be made for his accommodation and refreſhment; which Donna Urſula, the houſe-keeper, received with a heart burning with rage, and a face expreſſive at once of mortification and contempt.

Going from the great hall, Urſula was met in the paſſage by Father Thomas.—Here is rare work going forward, ſaid ſhe, in the great hall—I thought what would come of Don Iſidor's fooliſh orders—I ſuppoſe we ſhall have the place full of vermin—Why this is worſe again than the work he made about the three ragged raſcals of ſoldiers with the wooden legs.

Patience, patience, good madam! interrupted Father Thomas—What means this torrent of preſumptuous expreſſions to which you have given utterance? why thoſe unſeemly geſticulations and ſtrange marks of diſpleaſure?

Go into the parlour and ſee, replied the furious Urſula—There Don Alphonſo has got a beggarly old muſician in his honour's great chair, and has ordered breakfaſt for the fellow in as great ſtate as if he was a cavalier or a knight of St. Jago, although he has not got a maravedi's worth of clothes upon his back, and very likely, if he could get clear off, would rob the houſe of whatever he could lay his hands on.

Woman,

Woman, interrupted the reverend Thomas in a tone of ftern reproof, hold thy finful tongue, nor dare prefumptuoufly to give utterance to fuch expreffions in my hearing; obey with filent refpect the orders you have received; recollect that you are a fervant, and dare not to call in queftion the commands of him that feeds you: your want of charity demands a penance of another kind, which at a proper time I will not fail to exact; but your infolence now calls for the chaftifement which difobedient, faucy fervants deferve at the hands of their mafters: begone—do your duty, and let me hear no more of your comments on my noble child's conduct, or I vow I will fpeak to Don Ifidor on his return, and make him turn you to the world, and confign you for an exiftence to that charity which you would deny to others.

To be fure—as your Reverence fays, exclaimed the terrified Urfula.

Begone! I fay—and let me hear no more of it.

Thus faying, Father Thomas proceeded to the great hall. Upon his entrance Alphonfo fprang acrofs it, took him by the hand, and led him over to the old man, who immediately rofe, bent his aged knees, and befought his bleffing; which the holy man beftowed upon him, raifing him at the

same

fame time from the ground, and replacing him in the great chair.

Father Thomas then took a chair, feated himfelf, and, having furveyed the ftranger with an earneft and fcrutinizing eye, fighed, and preffed the hand of Alphonfo with a warmth expreffive of approbation; then addreffing himfelf to the old man, Have you travelled far this morning, Señor? faid he.

Only from the adjoining village, returned the other, where I was treated with a cheerfulnefs and hofpitality that would charm the ftubborn heart of mifanthropy itfelf, by a young man, who faid that he was, if I am not miftaken, one of this young gentleman's preceptors.

It is Juanico, cried Alphonfo in rapture—If Juanico was able, he would be as generous as the firft nobleman in Spain.

Alphonfo left the ftranger and Father Thomas in difcourfe, while he attended his duty in the menage—When that was difpatched, he impatiently returned, and found he had finifhed his breakfaft. The whole day he employed in fhewing him the gardens, woods, vineyards and caftle : the armoury particularly attracted the old man's attention—he looked with an eye of fkilful curiofity at every part, each in its turn. Do you not wifh,

my

my dear, faid he to Alphonfo, to be able to wear
thofe? I do very much, returned the youth; nay,
I am pretty fure that I am able even now; for
I can run with Sancho Perez, the biggeft boy
you faw with me, on my back, againft Juanico
who entertained you in the village; and I am
fure Sancho is twice as heavy as one of thefe.—
And why do you not try? interrogated the other.—
I am afraid, replied Alphonfo, that Don Ifidor
would fufpect me of vanity, and I know there is
nothing he hates fo much as vanity.—My dear,
my noble child, cried the Pilgrim, modefty like
yours fhould not go unrewarded; and if Don
Ifidor will deign to pay any attention to a poor
man like me, you fhall on his return have a trial.
—Ah, Sir, returned Alphonfo, my father regards
the poor as much as the rich, where he finds
them honeft and brave—but furely you are not
a poor man—I think you a very great man.—An
undefcribable fenfation thrilled to the old man's
heart. He feized Alphonfo in his arms, held him
for fome time clafped in his embrace, and wept.
Alphonfo wept too—he could not tell why—his
young heart was agitated with unaccuftomed fenfations of delight, and he fmiled through his tears:
the luftre of natural majefty broke through the
fable weeds that veiled it, and the dignified mind

C   of

of the youth, in eftimating the worth of his fel-
low-creature, laid no account on that of his
clothes.

Next morning, while Alphonfo and his new
friend were engaged in the armoury, the trampling
of horfes announced the arrival of Don Ifidor.
Father Thomas met and retired with him into
his clofet: as foon as permiffion was granted
him, Alphonfo flew to embrace his father: when
the mutual manifeftations of affection were
over, O father! faid Alphonfo, I have got you a
vifitor in the houfe.—So I have been told by Father Thomas, my dear; I entirely approve of
your behaviour to him, and thank you for fo very
honourably reprefenting me in my abfence: I am
the more pleafed with your attention to him, becaufe he is fo very poor a man.

Poor! repeated Alphonfo—furely, father, you
miftake—he is not poor—I never faw a grander
man in my life.

Do not depreciate your own charity, my dear,
faid Father Thomas—you cannot but have obferved the extreme poverty of his drefs.

His drefs! No indeed, faid Alphonfo, I took no
notice of his drefs: if it be poor, as you fay, I am
fure I am forry for it, for I cannot help loving
him. And turning to Don Ifidor, I refpect him as
                                                    much

much—almoſt as much as if it was yourſelf:—
then he has ſuch a commanding air—and he talks
ſo grandly of war, and honour, and courage,
and armour, that I am ſure he would delight
you.

What Alphonſo ſays is not entirely void of
foundation, ſaid Father Thomas.

Well, then, ſaid Don Iſidor, tell your friend
that I kiſs his hands, and ſhall be glad to ſee him
by and by in the great hall.

He is there now, Sir, ſaid Alphonſo; I hear the
ſound of his harp.

Then let us go to him, my dear.

On their entering into the hall the old man
roſe, and, with a deportment majeſtic beyond ex-
preſſion, ſaluted Don Iſidor; who, on his part, received him, not with that arrogant affectation of
humility which mortifies more than any other
exertion of pride, but with that unfeigned conde-
ſcenſion which made every benefit he conferred
valued leſs for the magnitude of the gift than the
cheerfulneſs of the giver. In truth, he felt in the
preſent caſe a veneration, if not awe, impoſed
upon him by the figure before him.

I will not, ſaid the old man, do ſo much injuſ-
tice to the character of Don Iſidor de Haro, as

to

to fuppofe, that the footing on which he finds a perfon of my humble appearance in his caftle will fubject Don Alphonfo to the imputation of rafhnefs, or me to the cenfure of forward intru-fion. Don Ifidor may be affured, that the kind-nefs of the youth (flattering though it was) fhould not have been accepted, had not univerfal report perfuaded me that it would have been approved by his father.

Venerable Señor, returned Don Ifidor, I hope you will find that your opinion, and the report which gave it birth, are not entirely mifplaced. My boy, whofe whole life has been one continued feries of acts the moft grateful to my feelings, has never done one more productive of fatisfaction to me, than procuring me the honour of your com-pany. I am not, continued he, a man of much ceremony, and fhall therefore only tell you, that my guefts are, to all intents of hofpitality, mafters of this caftle; and I beg that you will confider yourfelf fo. Do me the favour to take your feat, and I will again wait upon you as foon as I have given fome neceffary orders.

When Don Ifidor retired to his apartment he could not help reflecting on the extraordinary appearance of the ftranger. Pilgrims and itine-

rant

rant bards he had often feen, but never one that at all refembled this, in whom he imagined he could diftinguifh the remains of the warrior, and the defaced ruins of the man of dignity. That he was of a rank far above his prefent feeming, he had not the fmalleft doubt; but what that rank had been, or how he had fallen from it, he could not conceive, and he feared to enquire: even conjecture was loft in the wide field of calamitous events. While he was embarraffed in this confufion of thoughts, Alphonfo entered. There is fomething, my child, faid Don Ifidor, in this old veteran's manners, which exacts more than common refpect, and befpeaks him of fuperior rank, though fallen. I confefs an invincible curiofity to know who and what he is; but, as the recollection of fuch things muft be painful, I will rather content myfelf with ignorance of the matter than indulge my curiofity at the rifk of giving a fingle pang to his aged heart: I will therefore be filent on the fubject, unlefs he choofes of his own accord to difclofe himfelf to me. At all events, the great hall is a place where the difficulty he may have to be communicative muft be increafed by the frequent entrance of fervants. I wifh, my dear, to acquit myfelf to you of a vice which I have fo often

C 3

and

and fo vehemently reprobated to you, and therefore declare, that not idle curiofity, but an anxious
defire to heal, if poffible, the wounds that fortune
may have inflicted on him, induces me to this; I
will therefore direct one of the fervants to wait
upon him with my refpects, and inform him that
I fhall be obliged to him for his company in my
clofet.

Then, Sir, faid Alphonfo, I had better go myfelf: will it not appear more refpectful?

Thank you for your hint, my child, faid Don
Ifidor: you fpeak my very foul.

Alphonfo was not long away, when he returned
leading in the old man in the fame manner as he
had led him up the avenue. Don Ifidor was furprifed at perceiving that he had brought his harp
with him. Being feated, at the defire of Don
Ifidor, he proceeded, without a word, to tune his
harp, while his face exhibited marks of ftrong
emotions, and feemed pregnant with extraordinary
events. Don Ifidor would not break in upon him.
After a fhort prelude, he began to play, accom-
panying it with his voice. Melancholy had fet
her ftamp on every note he fung. Don Ifidor,
who heedfully attended, to catch from his verfes
a clue to his forrows, was for a time all ear.—

He

He fung of fortune and fame ruined, of friends and children loft, and of the miferies of an unconnected, ifolated exiftence here. Then he fung of war, till his harp, feeming to catch the enthufiafm of its mafter, ftruck fuch martial founds as roufed the blood of Don Ifidor, and filled the young Alphonfo with an ardour he was before a ftranger to. Hence he fkilfully turned to the happy ftate of Don Ifidor, whofe armour hung up at once a monument of its owner's former prowefs and prefent peaceful honours, and a leffon of emulation to the rifing fpirit of his fon. Don Ifidor at this part turned his eyes, which before had loft their functions in attention to the fong, on the old man, whofe face, glowing with the awakened enthufiafm of his fpirit, beamed with the glories of the warrior and the bard. In mute amazement he for a while gazed, tracing the lineaments of a countenance familiar to him, yet unknown—thrice he effayed to fpeak, but, loft in furmife, aftonifhment, and doubt, as often faltered. At length, with difficulty maftering the tumult within him, he faid, Ah, Sire! am I miftaken, or do I behold—do I fee the once beloved and ever revered —the glorious——Unfortunate Baron de Rayo! interrupted the old man.

Don

Don Ifidor had barely ftrength fufficient to rife and throw his arms about the Baron's neck—there, locked in a firm embrace, he held him for fome time, fpeechlefs with delight, while Alphonfo endeavoured to encircle both in his arms, kiffed the garments of both by turns, and wept and laughed together. At length Don Ifidor's great heart finding vent, he exclaimed—How, how is this?—Alas! alas! do I live to fee this day—the great Baron de Rayo, the glorious and the good—the plume of fcience, the thunderbolt of war!—Do I live to fee him thus?—do I live to fee my firft friend, my early director, he whofe inftruction and example firft called my youthful fpirit forth, pointed out the path to glory, and led the way to deeds of pith and virtue—divefted of his honours and diftinctions—travelling unattended, unaccommodated, like a minftrel, through the country!—Why, why is this? Penance it cannot be, for thy foul was as incapable of guilt as thy fpirit of difhonour. Say, then, my friend, my parent, how comes this to pafs? and why is the tranfport which I feel at thus finding thee reftored as it were from the dead, counterpoifed with the anguifh of feeing you thus fallen? Say, too, what of Gonfalvo, the dear companion of my youthful days?

All

All this time Alphonfo ftood in a gaze of wonder—the tears courfing each other in quick fuc-
ceffion down his cheeks.

Don Ifidor, faid the Baron, whatever my griefs
may be, I have yet room left in my bofom for a
large portion of joy to fee you once more, and to
fee you fo happy. Here Don Ifidor fhook his head.
—I fay again happy, continued the Baron. The
human mind, prone to difcontent, will, if it lack
real caufe of mifery, forge for itfelf ftings and
arrows out of the beft benefits of life. You have
had your afflictions, and I have fome conception
of them; but by the time you have heard my
tale, you will allow, that all the forrows you have
fuffered were joys, compared with mine. But fee
this tender lamb, his heart unufed to aught but
happinefs, fhrinks at the bare fuggeftion of our
woes; let us fpare him a recital which would only
fhock his gentle nature, and ferve no purpofe of
inftruction or utility. Another time——

My dear, faid Don Ifidor, fpeaking to Alphonfo,
could you not find fomething to amufe you for a
fhort time? ——

Yes, Sir, certainly, faid Alphonfo: there is a fuit
of armour below, which your noble gueft obferved
this morning would fit me; and, afking me if I
ever

ever had one on, and I telling him not, declared
he wifhed to be the firft to arm me. That, with
Don Ifidor's permiffion, I will go and get cleaned
up, that I may have the pleafure at once of trying
it, and conplying with our gueft's defire.

Which is it? faid Don Ifidor: is it mine?
Yours! Lord! no, Sir—it is the fmall one, the
French cavalier's.

Do as you pleafe, my dear, in this inftance; and
for the future, in all cafes in which this gentleman
directs you, remember that my advice or concurrence may be difpenfed with: go, then, my
child, and on what has juft now paffed between
my friend and me let your lips be fealed with
filence.

Alphonfo bowed in token of affent, and left
the room.

As foon as he was gone, It is an old obfervation, faid the Baron, conceived in wifdom and
founded on experience, that wherever there is
flattery there is a fool and a knave in the cafe. I,
for my part, think better of both of us than to
offer flattery, or expect it to be received: I fhall
therefore frankly declare, that in that youth, who
has now left us, Don Ifidor poffeffes a treafure
more than equivalent to all the loffes of his life.

Why

Why it is, I know not, but it is certainly a truth, that, from the inftant I beheld him, I felt myfelf fo tied to him by the ftrongeft cords of affeΩion, that to feparate him from me would be to tear every ligament of my heart afunder.—But I delay my promifed hiftory; and much I fear that the pain fome paffages of it cannot fail to give you, will be but poorly requited by the gratification of your curiofity.

CHAP.

C H A P. III.

The Baron's Relation.

ALPHONSO Baron de Rayo, thou well re-
memberest, was of no mean diſtinction—his caſtle
was as ſtrong, his wealth as great, his vaſſals as
numerous, as any peer's in the kingdom of Caſtile,
and his renown in war, and favour with his prince,
not leſs the topic of admiration with the nation at
large than the ſubject of envy to his enemies :—
his fortunes ſeemed founded on a rock, and his
honours and domeſtic circumſtances to bid defiance
to the ſtorms of adverſity—ſuch they were when
laſt we parted.

Heaven had ſpared me one daughter, the only
remaining child of a numerous progeny ; the reſt
followed their beauteous mother to the grave ere
yet they reached the years of puberty. This and
more thou already knoweſt ; but as it makes a
link in the great chain of events I propoſe to relate, I chooſe to be circumſtantial, even though it

ſhould

ſhould render me tedious. In the poſſeſſion of
that daughter, and the reſignation which, as a
Chriſtian, I owed to the will of Heaven, I buried
the remembrance of all my loſſes; and failing in
male iſſue, and being determined never to marry
again, I adopted the ſon of my ſiſter, the young
Henry Gonſalvo, reared him as my own, and
hoped, by my influence with the king, to get the
title and honours of the old houſe of Rayo entailed
upon him and his iſſue.

. At this time your father, the younger brother
of a reſpectable branch of our houſe, beſpoke my
patronage for you—I took you to my caſtle,
and, fancying that I ſaw in you the dawnings of
future greatneſs, determined to train you early
up to arms. Your progreſs and unfolding powers
juſtified my hopes; nor can I recollect many paſ-
ſages of my life that pleaſed me more than be-
holding, in the brotherly conteſts of emulation
between you and my Henry, the victory hang
now on this ſide now on that, till both were ex-
hauſted; for ſo perfect was the equality between
you at the cloſe of ten years, in which you continued together under my eye, that it remained
doubtful which excelled in vigour, dexterity, and
martial ardour; or which in tenderneſs, fidelity,
and mutual attachment. I looked upon you both
with

with pride—with hopes—and flattered myself that in each I saw a second self arising. But what was my exultation, when, our glorious king Alphonso calling me to the war against the Moors, I brought you both with me, and found that your actions exceeded my most sanguine expectation! The king, you know, on the taking of Algeziras, honoured you with knighthood, and gratified my fond wish by entailing the family honours and title on Henry Gonsalvo.

When our most beloved monarch, the friend and patron of our house, and the father of his people, died at the fatal siege of the Moorish fort Gibraltar, I retired in despondence and grief, and brought Gonsalvo with me; while you, arrested by a thirst for glory, and disdaining a life of inactive dependance, remained behind. We returned—Henry loaded with honours, and I exulting in the reflection, that the reputation of our family, for ages celebrated in the field, and distinguished for valour and loyalty, was likely to suffer no diminution in the hands of its new representative.

We had not been long at home, when I had the additional satisfaction to perceive an event ripening which I had from the first anxiously desired, and which alone was wanting to give full

3   com-

completion to all the wifhes or views I had on
this fide the grave: in fhort, I perceived that a
reciprocal affection was growing apace in the
bofoms of Gonfalvo and my daughter; and being
determined, neither on the one hand to injure
their love by anticipated concurrence, nor on the
other to throw any obftacles in their way by too
vigilant obfervation, I gave the young couple
juft as much time for uninterrupted communication
as I thought would ferve to ftrengthen their flame
without confuming their affection. Every thing
turned out correfpondent to my intentions. Henry,
fearful of the event, retired to his father's houfe,
and from thence gave me, by letter, a difclofure
of his paffion, with many expreffions of apprehenfion ; and above all, deprecating my fufpicions of
perfidy and breach of hofpitality in having paid
his addreffes privately to my daughter. I fpoke to
Maria with all the delicacy I could ; though I already knew, defired to be made the friendly confidant of her fentiments ; and affured her that my
confent fhould not be wanting to make her happy.
Overfpread with blufhes, and almoft finking with
apprehenfion and diffidence, fhe modeftly avowed
her love. O Ifidor ! her appearance, her manner,
her every word and look at that inftant recalled to
my mind the dear deceafed partner of my foul,
when

when blushing she gave herself to my arms.—
Here the Baron averted his face, and covering his
eyes with his hand, remained a few moments in silent agony. But recollecting himself, he exclaimed—This should not be—but sad remembrance
will obtrude itself.

A tear fell from Don Isidor, and the Baron resumed his story.

At this period Peter called forth all his forces
to crush a confederacy formed against him by some
discontented nobles, at the head of which were his
mother and his half brother. Peter was the legi-
timate son of our lamented king Alphonso; and
I thought it my duty to defend him, without examining the merits of his cause. Gonsalvo and
I accordingly set out to join the royal standard.
I will not enlarge upon the disgust the tyrant's
whole conduct gave us: it however served to
lessen, if not entirely remove the regret I felt at
finding that you had long been a follower of the
fortunes of Henry Count Transtamare, his brother.
You were right, as it has turned out; but I acted
upon principles of loyalty and allegiance, and find
my consolation in the consciousness of intentional
rectitude. To be succinct, we overcame the rebellion, and Gonsalvo and I returned to our peaceful
castle, with no other reward or compensation for

our

our pains than the laurels we gathered in the field, which, under such banners as we fought beneath, were withered ere they could be plucked.

Immediately on our return, the nuptials of my children were celebrated with all the pomp and dig-nity becoming their illuftrious houfe; and my happi-nefs foon received further augmentation by Henry's announcing to me the pregnancy of his wife. The wifhed for yet dreaded moment at length arriv-ed, and gave to our fond arms a noble boy : here my foul feemed to recline, and reft itfelf as after a long fatiguing journey. The child was fcarcely a minute from my fight—he was the delight of my foul—I hung in raptures over him, anticipat-ing the opening of his manhood, and drawing to myfelf, in fancy's flattering colours, the picture of his future form ; the vigour and fymmetry of thofe limbs, then in a ftate of fhapelefs, helplefs inaction; the fire of that fpirit then repofed in tor-pid apathy; and the varioufly expreffive beauties of that face, which then exhibited no trace of fenfa-tion, fave the tranfitory impreffions of accidental pain, or the paffing dimples of an unmeaning fmile.

A fhort time after this Peter again called us forth. His reiterated breaches of faith, his cruelties and exactions, raifed up againft him a formidable

D   power,

power, headed by Henry Count Tranſtamare, aſſiſted by the renowned Bertrand Gueſclin. I thought it our duty to attend him, nor could we, however willing at ſuch a time to remain at home, decline the ſummons without tarniſhing, or at leaſt hazarding our fame. We therefore prepared to depart; and the young child, which was named after me, Alphonſo, was put out to nurſe in a village near the caſtle, my daughter being determined to attend her huſband to Cordova. From this reſolution, however extraordinary, nothing could diſſuade her; and every thing being done that could render the journey convenient to her, we ſet out, and, without any incident worthy of relation, arrived at Cordova, which to our aſtoniſhment we found inveſted by Peter; his enormities having driven the inhabitants to the deſperate meaſure of declaring openly againſt him. We were, however, treated with every mark of diſtinction by the gentry round the place; and the ſingular heroiſm and conjugal affection of Maria raiſed her ſo high in every one's eſteem, and gained her ſuch univerſal reſpect, that her condition was rendered much more tolerable than we could poſſibly have hoped for.

Among thoſe who were moſt forward in doing honour to our family, was the Marquis de Punalada, a man of an illuſtrious houſe, and high in

favour

favour with the king: he had formerly been acquainted with Gonfalvo, and now renewed his intimacy with a zeal that gave us the more pleafure, as the capricious and violent temper of the king made the condition of all thofe who were not favourites, either immediately or collaterally, extremely precarious and difagreeable. We had little time for the cultivation of this intimacy. Henry was ordered off on a fervice of confiderable danger and difficulty; and I was ordered, together with all the elder barons, to remain with the army at the fiege, in order that the king might avail himfelf of our counfels—while Maria retired with the countefs Dalmado to the city of Eceja, to wait the return of her hufband.

I fhall not interrupt the thread of my ftory with a detail of the operations of the army, which perhaps you already know as well as I; but tell you, that here I was informed that you had perifhed with the other adherents of Count Tranftamare, with whom the tyrant broke faith fo wickedly at Toledo. Something, no doubt the ftings of a guilty confcience, fretted Peter, and inwardly preyed upon him: naturally ill-difpofed, he grew daily worfe, and the noble loyalty of fubjects never was put to fo fevere a trial as in adhering to the caufe of that weak, worthlefs tyrant.

For

For a confiderable time I had heard nothing from Gonfalvo or my daughter; I began to feel an uneafinefs unufual to me, at a neglect for which I was utterly unable to account, when one day I was put under arreft, and hurried before the king.

Unconfcious of having committed any offence to merit fuch a grofs indignity, I was bufied in forming conjectures on the ftrange event; when going through the camp to the king's pavilion, I heard a herald proclaiming my fon Henrico Gonfalvo a traitor. More at a lofs than before, I difmiffed the enquiry into the caufes from my mind, and only looked to the confequences, which I determined to endure with that unfhaken fortitude and dignity that became a noble Caftilian.

Arrived at the royal pavilion, I found Peter feated on his throne, a number of the nobility around him, and, as ufual, the Marquis de Punalada at his right hand, in conference with him, while his face appeared convulfed with a conflict of all the horrid paffions that fhake human nature, ftruggling for the maftery of his foul. Perceiving me, he turned abruptly from the Marquis de Punalada, and, addreffing himfelf to me, fternly faid—When foul rebellion ftains the branches of

a fa-

a family, and well-founded fufpicion falls upon
the chief ftock, what reparation does juftice to an
injured monarch demand—what meafures do his
fecurity require? Say, Baron de Rayo! I fpeak
to you.

When treafon or difloyalty is proved againft
the houfe of Rayo, my liege lord, returned I,
myfelf will be the firft, to pronounce the fentence of fevereft rigour, and call the execution
of it juftice.

That bafe diffimulation (interrupted Peter furioufly) which, under the plaufible pretext of rigour, and an affected zeal for juftice, affumes the
garb of innocence, but marks more ftrongly the
deep laid treachery of your views, and bids us
but the more beware of danger.

None, anfwered I, but the difloyal and treacherous ever found an enemy in, or had caufe to fear
danger from, our houfe—and who but your majefty
dares accufe us of it? Let the villain flanderer, be he
who he may, come forth, and my life fhall be the
pledge that I refute the calumny: and fure no
common calumniator it muft be, who could fhake
that confidence which the long and faithful fervices
of ages have juftly entitled the family of Rayo to
claim from the crown of Caftile.

Doft

Doſt thou then, diſſembler as thou art, interrupted the king, pretend ignorance ?· Why fled thy
rebel ſon, and joined the cauſe of Tranſtamare ?
Knoweſt thou nought of this ? or wilt thou pre-
ſume to ſay, that he who knew no thought but
thine, who moved but by thy guidance, and
yielded to no impulſe but the impulſe of thy ſpirit,
ſhould have taken ſuch a ſtep without thy knowledge and concurrence ? Thy nephew too pre-
ceded him in his rebellion : but he has paid the
forfeit of his crime, and ſo ſhalt thou ; we will
ſhew the proud Rayo that to offend us is ſome
danger, and that, as we raiſed, ſo we can lay his
honours in the duſt.

Gracious God! what was my indignation !—
Rage for ſome time deprived me of ſpeech, almoſt
of ſenſe. After ſome pauſe I rallied my ſcattered
ſenſes—The honours of Rayo, ſaid I, your majeſty has neither raiſed nor can extinguiſh—this
body, it is true, is in your power, and muſt endure
every outrage that jealous tyranny may chooſe to
inflict upon it; but the honours of myſelf and family ſhall mock thy threatened rage, ſoar beyond
the reach of thy poor revenge, and gain new vigour from the ſtrokes of perſecution.

Mark, cried Peter in a rage, mark ye, my
lords,

lords, the recreant defies us—Take him from our fight, and hurry him ftraight to prifon.

Yet, ere I go, faid I, let me, in prefence of thefe noble barons, exculpate myfelf from a charge the bare thoughts of which raife in my foul fcorn, abhorrence, and indignation. Here my feelings, like a torrent fuddenly contracted, overbore my reafon, and I added, Difclaiming all attachment and refpect to him who wrongs me, and aims a deadly blow at all my well-earned honours, I declare that merely to fatisfy my peers I ftoop to this vindication. Though Peter may have his own reafons for doubting the allegiance of any of his fubjects, the virtues of Rayo might fhield him from the charge of diffimulation.

I then turned to the knights and nobles. Peter, weak, wicked creature, biting his lips with internal agitation—My lord, faid I, why my fon has difappeared I cannot conjecture, nor did I know that event (if it has happened, which I yet doubt) till I came into this prefence: that he has gone over to the army of our adverfaries I cannot believe, as I know that his allegiance to the throne was equal to my own. Over this fome ftrange myftery hangs; a myftery which that God, who fees and knows the inmoft receffes of the heart, bears me witnefs I am utterly unable to get to the

bottom

bottom of: yet ftill I cannot believe that he would go and leave his wife a hoftage, for fure he loved her, and——

Mark the fubtle traitor, exclaimed the king— he would infinuate that he knew not of his daughter's flight.

My daughter! Mother of God, exclaimed I, is it poffible? What new wonders are yet for me to hear? what new myfteries to be unfolded? The barons feemed ftruck with my emotion.

Yet, my lords, rejoined I, let me turn to my own conduct, and fhew that I am abufed.

At the time that this war broke out, and the king called upon his people to rife in arms, my years might have exempted me, without imputation, from the fervices of war. Grown grey in the fervice of fucceffive kings, dignified with honours, and covered with the rewards of a monarch who knew how to eftimate my fervices, I might have ftayed at home and enjoyed the repofe neceffary to my years. Did I then come forth at thefe years to tarnifh all the glories of a well-fpent life, act the bafe diffembler's part, and play the hoary fool? I afk you, my lords, is it poffible? Yet am I without proof, enquiry, or even a full knowledge of the charge againft me, treated as a criminal, a criminal againft myfelf, my fortunes,

tunes, and my family. Obferve, my lords, how
this ftory hangs together: if we had determined
on the projeƈt of which we ftand accufed, what
hindered us from executing it in a manner and
at a time more fuitable to our views? Why delay
the defertion to that time and place which alone
could render it hazardous? Why fhould I be left
behind? The cloud of myftery which hangs over
it difqualifies me from fpeaking as I would do.—
But my part muft appear plain and manifeftly innocent; and as to my fon, I pledge my life for
his fidelity.

Here the king broke off my difcourfe; and,
rifing furioufly, ordered me into confinement. I
was hurried out of the pavilion, and the next day
was conduƈted under a ftrong guard, and lodged
a clofe and folitary prifoner in a cell in the tower
of Siguenca.

For a long time I was utterly incapable of re-
fleƈtion, or of entering into an inveftigation of
this unaccountable turn in our affairs: all within
was wild chaos, confufion, and uproar. Time
at length began to calm the perturbations of my
mind, and the tumults within gradually fubfided
into deliberation. I found myfelf, however, as
much at a lofs as before—In vain did I turn over
every incident of my life that could, by forced pof-

fibility, have given rife to the error ; all feemed more ftrange, unaccountable and inexplicable, the more it was examined ; and I had at length nothing left to think, but that my children, by fome means which I could not develop, had been facrificed to fraud and the fubtle defigns of fome hidden enemies, envious perhaps of the honours of our houfe.

O my Maria ! O my Henry ! would I exclaim, where are you, my comforts ? Do you ftill live, or has the ruffian hand of barbarous power affailed your precious lives ? O gracious Lord of all, if it be fo, give the guilty to the vengeance of thefe arms, old and withered though they be, and thy fervant will depart in peace !

Thus, day after day and month after month elapfed: having no diverfity of incidents to checquer exiftence, I had no objects by which to meafure time, and was uncertain what number of years I paffed in that dreary manfion. Lofing all hope of revifiting the world, I almoft loft all defire too, and had laid my account with ending my days in that difmal prifon ; when one night I was vifited by a dream or a vifion, and to this hour I cannot determine which. Methought, as I lay in my bed, Gonfalvo called to me. I looked up, and beheld

him

him pale, emaciated, with every appearance of wildnefs and diftraction in his face and air; I looked at him and wept; then ftretched forth my hands to embrace him : he eluded my endeavour. Alas! my fon, faid I, after fo long an abfence, is it denied me to——Sire, faid he, interrupting me, it availeth not—depart you hence, and feek my loft child. I effayed to fpeak, but could not—I endeavoured to call to him—he baffled all my efforts, and vanifhed, leaving me in an agony of confternation and grief.

Next morning the impreffion of this phantafm was fo ftrong upon my fenfes, that I was almoft at a lofs to determine whether it was a reality or a dream : while I was in a train of contemplation on it, the keeper of the prifon entered my chamber—I afked him whether any one had been admitted to me in the night—He faid, not; but at the fame time informed me, that he had that morning received orders to difcharge from confinement all perfons imprifoned there; Peter the Cruel being dead, and Henry Count Tranftamare, who killed the tyrant, having fucceeded to the throne.

The coincidence of the dream with this my deliverance made an impreffion on me difficult to conceive, impoffible to be defcribed. I thought

I faw

I faw the finger of Providence pointing out the way to fome ftrange and momentous revelation. The tumult of my feelings, furprife, joy, aftonifh-ment, and fufpenfe, was more than my enfeebled ftate could fupport. I was fcarcely able to move, and for fome days was unable to leave Siguenca; when at length I was able, I was at a lofs what way to go; but at laft determined to feek the Marquis de Punalada, of whofe friendfhip for Gon-falvo I entertained no doubt, and who would therefore be moft likely to give me information of his fate. With weary fteps I reached the city of Burgos : there I had the mortification to hear that my eftates were confifcated, and my blood attainted; and was moreover told, that the Mar-quis had quitted court, and retired to his eftate in Andalufia, long before the death of Peter. Thither, feeble and exhaufted though I was, I repaired—. After a long, wretched, and fatiguing journey, I reached a village near his caftle, and was told, that he then and moftly refided on his eftate on the banks of the river Ebro. I was furprifed at this intelligence, which neverthelefs was fufficiently confirmed by the people of the village. I deter-mined to find him. So recommending myfelf to the - Almighty, and befeeching him to endue me with ftrength and patience, I again turned my back on
Andalufia.

Andalusia. Not being able to travel in the state
suitable to my rank, the little means I possessed
being just exhausted, and moreover recollecting
that it might be prudent for me to pass as much as
possible unnoticed, I entered the town of Cordova,
equipped myself as you see, and then proceeded
on my journey, living occasionally at convents,
and on the beneficence of the hospitable people
of the country. My way was long; and as I
walked slowly, and was obliged to rest frequently,
it was a considerable time before I got to the
banks of the Ebro. The night before I reached
them I was visited by a dream nearly resembling
that which I had in the prison of Siguenca: Gonsalvo came in as before, and repeated the words,
Sire, seek my lost child! As before, I strove to
embrace him, when methought he turned from
me, uttering a sigh that seemed to shake his frame
to pieces.—We can no more, he said, and walked
away from me; when methought a ghastly wound
on his head yawned and discovered his brains,
and the blood ran in a torrent down his back.—My
soul, which till that minute was a stranger to the
impressions of fear, sunk with horror at the sight—
I trembled, gave a loud and hollow groan, and
awoke in an agony.—I ardently longed for the
return of day. It came, and brought no consolation—

tion—My dream had banifhed every gleam of comfort from my foul, and left nothing there but gloom, horror, and darknefs—yet fhall I own to you, that at intervals the pride of the warrior broke in upon my reveries, and painted to me imaginary profpects of revenge !

I traverfed the banks of the Ebro for many leagues, enquiring in vain for the Marquis de Punalada, till I came near that part which once owned me for its lord; a place I fhould above all others have avoided, were it not for the hopes of feeing my grandchild, or at leaft hearing of him—an indulgence which I deferred only for the purpofe of being firft fatisfied about his father and mother. As I approached, therefore, I felt all the torments of fufpenfe and apprehenfion. At length, however, I arrived within a fhort way of the caftle. It was evening when I knocked at the door of the firft peafant's cottage within the boundaries of the lordfhip of Montalto. A ftranger appeared, who rudely demanded my bufinefs. I told him I defired to fee Juan, the man of the houfe. If you mean Juan Navarro, returned he, you muft look for him fomewhere elfe. What, my friend, faid I, is not this his cottage? No, returned the clown; it was once his, but thank God and my mafter, it is mine now. And pray who is your

mafter ?

mafter? The Marquis de Punalada. The Marquis de Punalada! Yes, the Marquis de Punalada. The Baron de Rayo, its former owner, has been put to death for high treafon, and the king gave that caftle yonder, and this eftate, to my mafter: it is not above three days fince he left it, and went to his other eftate in Andalufia. O Heavens! what were my feelings!—how I fupported them I know not. The circumftance that Punalada, the fpecious· friend of Gonfalvo, rather, than any other perfon, fhould have got poffeffion of our confifcated property, ftruck like lightning a thought acrofs my mind, a fufpicion of an act too full of horror, guilt, and wickednefs, for man to perpetrate, and in the fulnefs of my heart I exclaimed, O curfed, curfed villain!—The fellow, full of refentment at my abufe (as I fuppofe he thought of himfelf), lifted his arm to ftrike me—I fmote him to the ground, and retired. Proceeding haftily to the next cottage, which was that in which my grandfon was nurfed, I received an anfwer there to nearly the fame effect.

Apprehending that the peafant, recovering, might collect a number of his lord's vaffals to affift him, and fall upon me, in which cafe refiftance or expoftulation would be equally vain, I turned into a wood, and, by a well-known path,
arrived

arrived at a village out of the power of the lord of the caſtle of Montalto; and calling at a cottage, took up my lodging for the night. Determined upon getting the beſt information I could, and above all to find out where my grandſon was lodged, I prevailed upon the ſon of my hoſt to go to the caſtle and the contiguous village, and make the neceſſary enquiries. He returned ſoon, and brought me an account that there was not one of the former inhabitants living on the lordſhip; that all were put out and replaced by ſtrangers, nor could it be found where any of them went.

You will allow that nothing could now be added to the meaſure of my afflictions, it was already running over. Loſt, then, I exclaimed—loſt indeed, my Gonſalvo! My Maria! loſt is thy child! I fear, yourſelves too! Where, ah where, bleſſed Father! ſhall my ſorrows end?—whither ſhall I go—where turn me to find my children, if yet they live?—Alas, I know not. Here, then, lay thee down, wretched old man, and patiently await the hand of death, which ſoon ſhall viſit thee and heal thy woes; or go to thy caſtle, aſſert thy right againſt the baſe vaſſals that poſſeſs it—ſlay all who oppoſe thee—till, thyſelf ſlain, thou ſhalt pull down a number to the grave with thee, and fall glori-

7   ouſly

oufly amidft the ruins of thy enemies! Here, ftifled with rage, and burfting with the fwellings of affliction, I fell on the floor in a ftate of infenfibility, to which a languor fucceeded that in all probability tended to fave me from the more acute effects of my paffion. The good people of the cottage, much affected with my emotions, ufed every little art to confole me, execrating the wretches who could aim a blow at a head fo white as mine. Urged by their repeated folicitations, I at length took fome food and went to bed: here, fleep, which ufually flies from the couch of the unhappy, led on by fatigue vifited me. Still I was haunted with the former dream, with little variation; and determined to purfue, as far as I could, the admonition. I therefore firft repaired to Toledo, to enquire of the chief officers of Henry Tranftamare's army, whether Gonfalvo had ever gone over; and after a moft minute inveftigation found that no fuch event had ever taken place: I thereupon refolved to commit myfelf to the direction of Providence, and fearch for my children, either till I found them or loft my life. Under this determination I firft vifited the court of Navarre, then that of Portugal; thence croffed Spain again over to the kingdom of Arragon: finding no trace any where of the objects of my purfuit, I formed the

E   defperate

defperate refolution of going to the Moorifh ter-
ritory of Grenada, on the bare poffibility of Gonfalvo's having been by fome unlucky means en-
flaved by the Infidels. Two years weary travelling, fupported by the alms of the charitable, could
not deter me from my purpofe : I therefore turned
my face that way, and proceeded, fupported by
the hope which the frequent vifitation of my dream
had infenfibly infpired me with. The fecond
night I took up my lodging among the charitable
fathers of a Francifcan monaftery. I informed
them of my intention, giving them at the fame time
my reafons for it, and difclofing to them the whole
of my misfortunes. One of them, a grave, wife
and learned man, undertook to diffuade me from
it : he remarked, that the difappearance of my fon
and daughter happened in a place and at a time
that the Moors could not, by any poffibility, have
been inftrumental to it : he faid, that he thought
the much greater probability was, that they had
been, for fome hidden purpofe, cut off by the cruel
hand of Peter ; and that by going to Grenada, I
fhould only bring down additional mifery on myfelf, and lofe the fmall probability there was of recovering or finding out my grandchild ; and he
finally advifed (in which all agreed with him)
that I fhould rather go to Toledo, apply to the

Arch-

Archbifhop, and through him get an order of go-
vernment to fearch for them. I perceived that
the eagernefs of my defires had confounded my
judgment, and that I had, in the flame of purfuit,
overlooked feveral material objections to my plan.
That night I went to bed, undecided in my
intentions; ftill I was vifited with the dream—
Gonfalvo again fhewed his cloven fkull, and again
urged my departure in fearch of his child. Alas!
my child, faid I, whither fhall I go? Go, faid he,
fate will inftruct thee and guide thy fteps. Methought I immediately went forth on the defired
fearch—I walked with difficulty up a fteep hill: at
length I thought I got into a field where two armies
were drawn out in preparation for engagement;
the trumpets founded a charge, the martial clangor
filled my foul with a tranfport not to be defcribed;
I wielded my lance, and was hefitating which fide
of the fcales I fhould throw my weight into, when
methought you, Sir Ifidor, ftept forward, cafed
in full armour, you came forward to me and faid,
Noble Rayo, Ifidor de Haro will give your children to your arms or perifh in the attempt: with
that I thought you vanifhed, but foon returned,
and advancing towards me fmiling, prefented me
a golden helmet in which was laid my child, my
Alphonfo: I fuddenly grafped the helmet, and

E 2   fnatched

snatched the child to my bosom, when looking down, I perceived that the helmet falling had killed his father, who lay bleeding in agony on the ground. My woe and horror were unutterable : I turned the point of my javelin towards my breast, determined to rush upon it, when methought you held me, and struggling with me, snatched the fatal weapon from my hand, and said, Grieve not, be patient, all shall yet be well, I will be myself a father to Alphonso. In endeavouring to throw my arms about you I awoke.

This new dream furnished my heated imagination with new materials to work upon; a train of new ideas took place, and a new plan arose from them. Perhaps, thought I, Isidor may yet live—perhaps uncorrupted too.—I will seek him out thought I, and leave the rest to the great Disposer of events.

I arose early next morning and set forward on my way to the court of Henry, with an intention to ascertain the fact, whether you were dead or not ; and I confess I was startled at the apparent past derangement of my mind, which could so long have dwelt upon my misery without thinking of so obvious a remedy as this probably offered. I travelled some days, when accidentally passing through your village, I chanced to hear your name

mentioned

mentioned in fuch terms as convinced me, that I was near the habitation of a friend : and now I am here, I muft confefs that I find myfelf, I know not why, in a ftate of more internal compofure than I have for years been accuftomed to ; and weak though it may appear to you, the frequent vifitations of Gonfalvo, and his injunctions in the dream, and the fubfequent one, in which you appeared, coupled with the circumftance of meeting you, the name and perfonal appearance of this lovely youth, together with a confufed crowd of other ideas, rufh on my mind with a force which reafon cannot refift. Here he paufed, and fixing his eyes fteadily on Don Ifidor, as if to catch every paffage of his mind through his eyes, he continued—Tell me, Ifidor, in pity to a father's feelings tell me, knoweft thou, or haft thou heard ought of Gonfalvo or of my daughter ? and oh fay, nor delay to folve the torturing doubts of my wretched care-worn heart—fay—Who is this youth—this Alphonfo ? Oh fay ! for much my mind mifgives me—and fure if I be miftaken the ftrong refemblance warrants me : in him Gonfalvo all appears in renovated youth, moves in every ftep, and fpeaks in every fentence that he utters.

Don Ifidor, ftruck with aftonifhment at the conclufion of this ftory, ftared for fome time at

the

the Baron, transfixed in filence. If the misfortunes of a family he fo entirely loved, affected him with forrow, the whimfical tranfition from it to his fon fmote him to the foul : he loved the Baron with more than filial tendernefs, and as he always admired him for his extraordinary valour, fo he revered him for his fuperior wifdom ; but to fee his foul fo fhaken, and his underftanding fo enfeebled as to yield up his reafon to the mere illufions of fancy, and to fuffer his judgment to be fo tainted by the falfe colourings of a dream as to call in queftion his property in his own child, fhocked him beyond meafure. The refemblance his fon bore to Gonfalvo he had himfelf noticed, and with pleafure noticed, as it ferved to keep up the remembrance of a much loved, long loft friend and relation : but the Baron's ftraining that refemblance to a conclufion fo wild and extravagant, was a falling off too lamentable not to overwhelm him with grief and aftonifhment. Unable from thofe impreffions on his feelings to fpeak, he for fome moments continued filent, his face imprinted with the ftrongeft marks of concern—while the Baron's hope, gaining new ftrength from the paufe, caft a vifible gleam of fatisfaction over his countenance.

My dear Lord, and moft valued friend, faid he,

after

after fome hefitation, to fay that your misfortunes affect me as though they were my own, and that there is nothing within the compafs of my power which I would not do to redrefs or relieve you from them, is to fpeak far fhort of my feelings and inclinations, and is no more than, I truft, you will readily believe: would to heaven that the remedy were immediately to follow the effort, and fleep fhould not feal my eyelids ere you found it. In the difappearance of Gonfalvo, my lofs is not lefs, nor did my grief fall fhort of yours; but, with the extinction of hope, my grief has abated; I have long ceafed to think that he lives; fome account of him elfe muft furely long fince have reached his friends; but as to the mode or caufe of his difappearance, I find myfelf as unable to form even a vague conjecture as you can be. As to the reft, hear my ftory and be fatisfied.

E 4   CHAP.

CHAP. VIII.

Don Isidor relates his History.

YOU may remember that, previous to our going against Algeziras, we were entertained at the court of Alphonso, then at Burgos, and treated with uncommon marks of diftinction ; there was a vaft concourfe of nobility there, as well thofe who were going to the war, as their friends and relations, who came to fpend as much time as poffible with them before their departure, and bid them a final adieu—Don Alvarez de Guzman was at that time the King's chief favourite, and of courfe the moft confiderable perfon prefent. The pomp and dignity of this great man's family contributed to the fplendour of the court, but no part of it fo much as his fair niece Donna Ifabella de Guzman, who feemed to engrofs the eyes and admiration of the court, and to eclipfe all the young ladies then prefent ; though there were many of the firft in eftimation both for birth and beauty in the train of the Queen Maria. As Gon-

7   falvo

falvo and I ftood in a familiar degree of intimacy
with Don Alvarez, I had frequent opportunities
of converfing with Donna Ifabella, and found that
her mind was as highly gifted with wit, and en-
riched with knowledge, as her perfon was with
beauty—Not to trouble you with a detail of minute circumftances interefting only to the parties
concerned ; we conceived a reciprocal tendernefs
for each other, and I obtained her confent to demand her in marriage from her father, and to that
end to afk the affiftance of Don Alvarez ; but as
her father was of a very high rank and proud difpofition, and I at the time but a foldier of fortune, it was determined that I fhould wait till my
fervices entitled me to rank, which in the fcene
we were then going to, was likely foon to happen.
We privately plighted our faith to each other, and
parted with mutual affurances of eternal and
inviolable fidelity.— Soon after we took the field :
what happened there, and afterwards at Gibraltar
up to the time of your departure, I need not mention ; the King, you know, honoured me with
knighthood, and on your returning home I refolved to remain with the army returning back to
Caftile, actuated perhaps by a thirft for glory,
but certainly by my paffion for the fair Ifabella too.
And here, my lord, it may be proper to make an
excufe

excufe to you, for a concealment that favours too
ftrongly of infincerity. My duty to you, who was
more than a father to me, and the confidence
which your friendfhip intitled you to, demanded a
communication of fo very important an affair ;
but the truth is, I was doubtful of fuccefs, and
too proud to circulate the fhame (as I then
thought it) of a difappointment if I fhould fail:
let it fatisfy you, that I did not communicate it
even to Gonfalvo.—But to return whence I have
digreffed : I thought my newly acquired honours
gave me more reafonable pretenfions, and made
this a fit feafon to introduce the fubject of my
paffion to Alvarez, not doubting from the ftrong
friendfhip he expreffed for me, and which I
thought was fincere, that he would willingly
render me all the fervice he could on the occafion.
Whatever his private feelings on my opening the
bufinefs to him might have been, he affected to
take my propofal in good part, but told me that
to the King and Queen Dowager Maria I muft
make my fuit, as they had honoured the young
lady with their patronage, and had taken to
themfelves the tafk of providing for her a fuitable alliance.

The duplicity of Alvarez muft have been
obvious to any one, who was not blinded by

excefs

excefs of paffion on one hand, and the fecurity of fincere friendfhip on the other. I thought he was fincere; whereas if I had only taken the pains to reflect, I might have feen that he fhould have taken the office of opening the matter to the King upon himfelf. However, as I ftood tolerably well with Peter, I felt little repugnance to difclofe my inclinations to him, which I did the fucceeding day in the modefteft 'manner I could, concluding with an account of our reciprocal attachment, and of our engagement to each other, which we had entered into previous to my taking the field.

I was much furprifed to fee the King knit his brows, and difcover manifeft marks of difpleafure during the latter part of my fpeech.—When I had done, Don Ifidor de Haro, faid he, we have been pleafed with thy fervices to our royal father, and have given thee proofs of our approbation—but think no more of this lady as you value our favour —we have already provided her with a fuitable match—our royal word is pledged, and cannot be departed from. I ventured to remonftrate, but he was inflexible, and I left his prefence in a ftate, compared with which the ordinary miferies of life were comfort. I fought Alvarez, and he told me that he was from the beginning apprehenfive that I fhould not fucceed, for that he had reafon to

believe

believe the king purpofed marrying her into the noble family of Garcias.

With all the diffimulation of a true courtier, Don Alvarez affected to condole with me on my misfortune; and I left him, nothing relieved by his difcourfe, though full of gratitude for his friendly fympathy.

The agitation I was thrown into by this mortifying refufal affected me fo violently, that I was taken extremely ill of a fever, the caufe of which my pride urged me to keep concealed. In this extremity I had nothing to fupport or relieve me but my dependence on the fidelity of my Ifabella, whofe foul was far above falfehood or caprice; and the indefatigable attention of my faithful fervant Pierrot; who, in his grief and care for me, brought himfelf into a ftate of health little better than my own. Thus was I nearly reduced to all the horrors of ficknefs, folitude, and difappointed paffion. What, thought I, avail my newly-acquired titles?—I am a ftep of honour higher it is true, but all my hopes of happinefs are perhaps for ever blafted!—Titles, rank, and all the pride of man, what are you but deceit?—you mock mifery, point the fting of adverfity, and hold out the horrors of ruin to our view in tenfold amplification!—In fhort, I not only forgot my honours,

but

but myself also, and lived for some time almost unconscious of existence.

I was roused from this state of torpid despair by an account that Peter was preparing to arm against our present king, then Count Transtamare. 'The news struck a gleam of light acrofs my mind —love suggested hope, and pride whispered revenge. I had known Henry during the life of Alphonso; we had often conversed and hunted together, and he professed a strong friendship for me, as well as for Gonsalvo: you will not wonder then, that the character of Peter, the insult he had already offered, and those which it was probable I might yet receive at his hands, joined to my respect and love for Henry, should of themselves, even exclusive of my passion for the fair Isabella, suggest to me the idea of deserting the service of the tyrant and flying to that of his adverfary.—— The thought no sooner occurred than my resolution was taken, and I only waited for an opportunity of once more seeing my Isabella, to carry it into execution. This opportunity foon offered. I informed her of the king's refolution—of my determination to retire and wait for a more favourable time to complete our wifhes: I conjured her to be firm in rejecting any propofals of marriage from another quarter, and assured her that

it

it was my determination to take her from under the tyrant's power or perifh in the attempt. She anfwered, that it was probable that would be effected without my interference, as the Queen Mother, Maria, in whofe fuite fhe was, was at the head of the confederacy formed againft Peter, and in league with Count Tranftamare : and, finally, fhe affured me, that nothing but-death, or my own inclination, fhould keep us from uniting our fates together.—We knelt down together, and with the holy rofary and crucifix clafped in our hands, fwore to each other mutual fidelity. That very evening I departed, attended by my faithful Pierrot, whofe joy at getting fairly out of Peter's reach, which happened abont fun-rife the enfuing morning, burft forth in a train of fongs, jefts, and obfervations, fo fimple, fo pleafant, and fo natural, that my gloomy reflections were infenfibly banifhed from my heart ; and I felt a tranfport the more exquifite as it was fo long a ftranger to me.

When I reached Toro, where Henry was affembling his forces, he received me with open arms, expreffed an earneft wifh that Baron Rayo and Gonfalvo would fhake off their attachment to the tyrant and join him ; but affured me, that as he well knew the refined principle upon which the

Baron

Baron adhered to the reigning monarch, and the rigid honour and integrity which governed his actions—let the event of this conteft be what it would, he and his family fhould be protected. Not to detain you with a recital of events which you know as well as me, the fall of Toledo was the fate of our caufe; I efcaped out of it by miracle; and, ftill attended by my faithful Pierrot, bent my courfe towards Portugal. The extreme fatigue of my body, joined to the anxiety of my mind, brought me again fo low, that I was obliged to take up my lodgings at a peafant's cottage on the banks of the river Guadiana : here the genial temperature of the air, the wholefome fimple diet, the uninterrupted repofe of the cottage and its inhabitants, whofe cheerfulnefs infenfibly found its way to my heart, and above all, the exertions of my faithful Pierrot to entertain and ferve me, facilitated my recovery, and made a confiderable alteration in my fpirits. I foon had ftrength to bathe and to hunt in the woods; and, pleafed with the daily increafe of my health and ftrength, remained there till I was perfectly recovered.

It was not without great regret that I quitted this fweet humble abode of innocence, hofpitality, and pleafure; after making the cottagers the beft return I could for their hofpitality, we feparated,

not

not without emotions of forrow on all fides. I
thought that Pierrot would have broken his heart;
and nothing lefs than his attachment to me could
have torn him from them. Ah, your honour,
faid he, as we travelled along, that is what may
be called living—that is a life after God's own
heart—there we were neither afraid of crafty un-
dermining rivals, falfe friends, or cunning cour-
tiers; there we had neither envy, jealoufy, fraud,
nor diffimulation; there we could lie down in our
beds without any apprehenfion of death but fuch
as the Almighty might be pleafed to vifit us with
—without any fear of being one day pufhed into
the field of battle, and next day upon the fcaffold
—there were no tyrants to cut us off—no Peter
to rob us of our fweethearts.

This laft word roufed me from a ftate of repofe
in which the unufual calmnefs of our life at the
cottage, and the exhilarating influence of returning
vigour had laid me. I relapfed into reflection—I began again to feel all the mifery of being thus tyran-
nically cut off from every thing that could render
life fupportable to me; I was ftung to the quick
at the thoughts of Ifabella's being put into the hands
of a rival; and as ftrength increafed, the vigour of
my mind increafing alfo, I began to examine the
grounds of my defpondence, and found that much

of

of it was owing to a momentary awe, impreſſed upon me by the furious and known relentleſs nature of the tyrant Peter, and the conſequent depreſſion of my ſpirits : I began to cenſure my too eaſy acquieſcence, bluſhed for the meanneſs of my conduct, and heartily ſcorned myſelf for the abject dereliction of the duty I owed to my own happineſs, and to the faith I plighted to my Iſabella. All allegiance to Peter was caſt off—my fortunes were inſeparably connected with thoſe of Tranſtamare, which, though at preſent clouded, were far from extinguiſhed, the wickedneſs of Peter himſelf being a more powerful engine in his favour than all the hoſts of France. With this proſpect, ſuch as it was, I thought I could be content, could I only get poſſeſſion of my Iſabella. I ſhould have told you, that on the rupture between the Queen Mother and Peter, ſhe retired to her father's houſe : one difficulty only therefore lay in my way, but that was to all appearance an almoſt inſuperable one ; the probability being, that as Peter had cruſhed the confederacy, her father would not merely refuſe his conſent, but uſe every ſtratagem to deliver me up to the tyrant : I determined, however, to leave no means uneſſayed on my part, and to truſt the reſt to the affection of my Iſabella and the direction of Providence.

F   Having.

Having thus adjusted the matter in my mind, I recrossed the Guadiana, and, disguised in the dress of a common Pisano, turned by the most unfrequented ways back through Spain towards Talavera, at a small distance from which, but where particularly I did not know, her father had his abode. After some days weary travelling, I found myself near Talavera; and, in order to get proper information, determined to stop at the first cottage I came to. It was not long till one offered of a most inviting appearance; with the cheerful consent of the people I dismounted from my horse and entered, and found it within clean and well accommodated, beyond any thing I could have hoped for or had ever seen with peasants. After eating a hearty dinner I retired to a small room to repose me, after the fatigues of the journey, and soon fell into a profound sleep. I had not enjoyed it long, when I was awakened by a hand shaking me by the shoulder, rather roughly. Surprised, I looked up, and saw Pierrot hanging over me with a face in which the most whimsical mixture of various expressions was pourtrayed: joy, however, was the predominant trait, and I was pleased before I had reason to think I had cause to be so. Lord, your honour! says he, I hope you will pardon my waking you; but I could not for the life

of

of me refrain—O bleſſed Virgin! Can you think
it—the ſtrangeſt, luckieſt, oddeſt affair!—What!
exclaimed I—prithee ſay what it is? Oh, your
honour! I am half dead with joy, for to be ſure
nobody could have expected it—Did not I tell
your honour how I dreamed laſt night that the
horſe you rode was all on fire under you, and yet
never conſumed or burned? and did not I tell
you that it was a bleſſed dream, and that luck
would come of it? And did not I tell you——
What—indefatigable babbler! what is it you
would tell me? Well, well, ſay what you will,
dreams come out as true as the goſpel of St. John
of God. For Heaven's ſake, Pierrot, have you
a mind to rack my brain to pieces with ſuſpenſe,
and make it as wild as your own? Tell me
quickly what you mean, or by Heaven!—Well,
to be ſure, if 'I thought your worſhip would be
angry, my throat ſhould have burſt with the ſtory
or e'er I ſhould have diſturbed you: God knows,
I thought that you would have flown through the
roof of the houſe, like a ſpark of fire up a chim-
ney, at the very mention of it. Hear me, Pierrot,
ſaid I haſtily—If you have aught that concerns
my peace, which, by the wildneſs of your looks,
and the incoherence of your words, I am inclined
to believe, let me have it in three words, or here

F 2   I abjure

I abjure you. Three words, indeed—three words!
rejoined Pierrot, Lord of Heaven help you—it is
worth three thoufand words! But what are words?
—Three thoufand pieces of gold—three thoufand
rubies and emeralds would be too cheap a pur-
chafe for fuch good—fuch delightful——Begone!
faid I, in a rage—Fly! before I am tempted to
commit fome rafh action and annihilate you on
the fpot—brute—afs—barbarian! Here I rofe up
in the bed, and, lifting up a chair, was going to let
it fly at him, when he walked away, muttering to
himfelf, and, getting outfide the door, and half
thrufting in his head, with a look of arch reproach,
he faid—You are too angry then to hear news of
my Lady Ifabella? Gracious God! exclaimed I,
leaping from my bed—Lady Ifabella! Say again—
Where? How? In what way? Tell me—tell me
all. Aha! faid he triumphantly, ecod I thought
your honour was not quite awake at firft, or you
would not have made fuch a difficulty of hearing
my ftory. You muft know, then, that in this
very houfe, this that we now are in, and in that
very bed in which you juft now lay, and by that
clean, orderly, neat, good-looking old body of a
woman, that you faw fitting in the wicker chair
(well, happy was her lot, and fhe fays fo herfelf)—
'Sdeath! What of her? There now again—you

cannot

cannot have patience, and I telling you in as few
words as poffible—by her then was your noble, dear,
charming Lady Ifabella nurfed. Mother of Mercy,
is it poffible!—Poffible! Is my name Pierrot?—
As fure then as it is my name, fo true is what I
fay: nay, this very morning did fhe blefs this cottage with her prefence; and, to-morrow morning
will come again; nay, if good luck befal, fhe may
be here perhaps this evening, for it is yet far
from night, and fhe fometimes comes after dinner.

In a fit of rapture, I threw my arms round my
faithful Pierrot, whofe joy was nearly as great as
my own, and who, while I was dreffing myfelf,
told me, in his disjointed confequential manner,
at which I fhould on another occafion have laughed, that the nurfe mentioning her young lady's
name, and he afking her, if fhe ever heard of
mine, declared, that I had been almoft the only
fubject of converfation between them for fome
time; and that fhe fpoke of me as of a perfon already her hufband.

This account made me think that I fhould run
no hazard in informing the old woman who I
was: I called her therefore into the room, and
told her—fhe wept for joy, and declared it was
the happieft event fhe had for a long time known,

as

as she was sure it would render her child (so she called my Isabella) completely blest. She had not long retired, when we heard the outer door open, and a person enter—a confused, indistinct buzzing of female voices succeeded, and continued for some minutes; at length I heard a well-known voice—a voice more ravishing to my ears than seraphs' songs. Is it possible! gracious God, is it possible! Is my Isidor in this house?—Unable to contain myself, I burst from the room and caught her in my arms—Yes, my love, my faithful, my adored Isabella, your Isidor is here; and this blessed, joyful interview is more than recompensed for ages of affliction. Oh my Isabella, didst thou but know what pangs, what sufferings mine have been!

Here I was interrupted by the old woman with, I do not know, young Señor, what your sufferings may have been, but many and many a tear has my young lady here, in this very spot, shed over your name; and even I, who did not know you, was fain to keep her company—she did so take on—But, Lord, Sir! I hope you will go fighting no more—fighting is a woundy mischievous, unchristianlike thing, and no luck can come of it; and then my lady trembles so at the very thoughts of it, that I wonder how you could have the heart to set about it.

The

The old woman's gabble was a very seasonable relief to Isabella, who had sunk into my arms in a soft, speechless delirium of joy and surprise.—As soon as cool reflection resumed its seat, I told her every thing that occurred, as I have already told it to you, and desired her advice upon the steps necessary to be taken to insure our happiness. The division between Queen Maria and her son Peter, she said, had not altered the intention of the latter: and she candidly confessed, that she had received her father's positive commands to entertain Garcias as her husband: that she was convinced all attempts to alter his resolution would be vain, and that my discovering myself would certainly be attended with utter ruin. Under those circumstances, she said she was at a loss what to advise—but knowing my honour, and convinced of my sincerity and affection, was willing to adopt any measure that I should prescribe to her.

We now called the old nurse into consultation, and after some deliberation it was agreed, that we should be married the next morning at the cottage, and that the ensuing night she should leave her father's unobserved and join me at the cottage, whence we should immediately depart, and take shelter in Arragon, till I could get intelli-

gence

gence where Count Tranſtamare had diſpoſed of himſelf.

Early next morning the old woman diſpatched her huſband to a neighbouring village for a prieſt, who lived there, to prevail on him to come to the cottage and perform the ceremony; and, in the mean time, ſent away a young lad, her ſon, to the town of Talavera, under pretence of getting medicines for her gueſt, who feigned ſickneſs for the purpoſe, in order that he ſhould be no interruption, nor ſuſpect what was going forward. The old man being properly qualified to apply to the feelings of the prieſt, that is to ſay, having a purſe well ſtocked with money, readily obtained his conſent, and they both were betimes in the cottage to breakfaſt. Nothing was wanting now but the bride: with eager eyes I traced the path ſhe was to come—I grew uneaſy—then impatient —at laſt my heart ſunk into deſpair.—At length ſhe appeared—Oh my Iſabella! ſaid I, in a tone of tender reproach, my heart was dying within me—the day was ſo far advanced, I began to fear you were detained. Thou dear impatient, ſaid ſhe, doſt thou know that it is not yet eight o'clock? Such are the thorny feelings, ſuch the hopes and fears of true love. But why do I trouble you with a fooliſh detail of uſeleſs unintereſting trifles?

Oh,

Oh, proceed with it, said the Baron—be
minute, be particular—the moſt refined intellec-
tual ſenſation, the moſt exquiſite delight, is that
which ariſes from a nice inveſtigation of the virtuous paſſions. Always an admirer of beauty—
always the friend of love—age has not diminiſhed
my admiration of the one, nor my eſteem for the
other ; and I declare, that no part of your ſtory
has afforded me ſo much pleaſure as the deſcription of your paſſion and fondneſſes with your amiable Iſabella.

Ah, Baron! returned Don Iſidor, amiable indeed! had you but known her—had that bliſs
but been reſerved for me, to ſee you claſp her in
your fond parental arms, and beſtow your bleſſing.

Hold, Iſidor, interrupted the Baron—Have I
not griefs enough already? Would'ſt thou that
this too was added to the load ? Alas ! I fear, nay
I feel, that I ſhall but too much deplore her loſs
upon the ſtrength of thy deſcription ; to loſe her,
when known, might have been too much:—but
go on, my child! I interrupt you.

To proceed, we were married in preſence of
the old couple, their daughter, who attended on
Iſabella, and my honeſt Pierrot ; who, perhaps, in
exceſs of joy fell not ſhort of ourſelves : he muſed,

he

he capered, he cried and laughed alternately; and
when the knot was tied, his reafon overcome by
the overflowing of his heart, he dropped on his
knees at Ifabella's feet, and, fnatching her hand,
kiffed it as if he would devour it—wept till he
wetted it—and called her his mafter's faviour!

The prieft gave me a proper certificate of our
marriage, and departed, after having given us the
moft folemn affurances of fecrecy. Ifabella returned to her father's houfe, and I retired to my
room in a ftate of delicious tranfport that I was
before a ftranger to. I fpent the reft of the day
in framing plans of future happinefs for myfelf and
my Ifabella.

Impatiently did I wifh for night—it at length
came, and in due time brought my treafure to my
arms.—We fet out without lofs of time; Ifabella
mounted on my horfe, while I rode on that of
Pierrot, and he and Ines, my wife's attendant, on a
mule purchafed of the old man for the purpofe.

I thought it moft advifable to take the fhorteft
road poffible out of Peter's dominions, and therefore ftruck into one that led to the kingdom of
Arragon: we arrived without any material accident at the city of Saragoffa, where a rumour was
in circulation, that there was immediately expected a rupture between the kingdoms of Caftile
and

and Arragon. I directly difpatched an account of
this to the Count Tranftamare, then taking refuge
at the court of France, in order that he might turn
the rupture to the moft advantageous account his
policy might fuggeft to him. It was not long
after that Henry himfelf appeared at Saragoffa,
entered into a league with the King of Arragon,
and took the field once more againft Peter. The
prudence and valour of Henry gave victory to the
Arragonian troops wherever he led them. I was
feldom from his fide, and can fay that no man
ever deferved good fortune better; for, as none
fhewed greater power in winning her over, fo none
ever made a better ufe of her when won. The
war was very fuccefsful: however, the King of
Arragon thought proper to patch up a peace with
Peter, and Henry conceiving it prudent not to
confide too far in him, returned again to Paris,
attended by his wife Joanna, who had been refcued
from the tyrant's hands, and by me and my
Ifabella.

While we were in Arragon my wife was deli-
ved of a fon—that fame boy whom you honour
with your regard—Henry was his godfather, and
with my confent named him Alphonfo in honour
of the King his father's memory. His mother
being extremely ill and weak after her lying-in, it.

was thought expedient to put the child out to
nurfe; and as we were to go into France, and it
was neceffary to leave the child behind, we difpatched Pierrot to Ifabella's old nurfe at Talavera,
to procure one fhe could depend on there in order
to be under her eye. The child accordingly was
given to the woman fent by her with Pierrot,
and who went back attended again by him, fur-
nifhed with a fufficient fum for three years expences to be delivered to the old woman for dif-
burfement.

The anguifh at parting with this dear firft
pledge of our loves was unutterable; my wife's
particularly was fo extreme that fhe could
fcarcely fupport it, and fhe proceeded to Paris
with a heart foreboding an eternal feparation from
her child.

Of the various fortunes of Count Tranftamare,
in his ftruggling for the throne with Peter, as
you muft already know them, I need not inform
you, more particularly as it would break in upon
the thread of my ftory; fuffice it to fay, I was
with him in all, and even when domeftic forrow
made me unfit for the world I attended him.

The fun of my bridal rofe with brightnefs, but
was, alas! eclipfed in its meridian—My wife had
two children in the three years following the birth

6

of

of Alphonſo, who both died infants : in the fifth year ſhe again proved pregnant—fatally pregnant —in due time ſhe had a daughter who cloſed the ſcene, for in nine days after its birth I loſt my comfort, my peace, my all, in Iſabella—ſhe died and left me the moſt miſerable of all created beings. Yes, yes! all joy vaniſhed with my Iſabella!—Here Don Iſidor ſtopped, haſtily aroſe from his ſeat, and retired. The good old Baron, who ſaw and participated in his affliction, patiently ſat with brim-full eyes in expectation of his return. At length Don Iſidor came back—took his ſeat— gave the Baron a ſqueeze by the hand, with a look ſoliciting pity, and endeavoured to proceed—— The Baron purpoſely interrupted him, Did you hear nothing of your wife's father all this time, and did Don Alvarez take no ſteps to mediate between you and his brother ?—I ſhould have told you in its proper place, that my wife opened to me the whole artifice and duplicity of Alvarez : it was at his inſtigation that the King reſolved to marry her to Garcias, and ſhe incurred his reſentment by her reſiſtance.

When Iſabella was brought to bed of her firſt child, I wrote to her father to inform him of the event, beſeeching his bleſſing for his daughter and her child ; he ſent me a reply groſs and rude to

the

the laſt degree, diſclaiming all connection with his
daughter, and threatening me with the utmoſt
vengeance of the King. I deſpiſed the threat as
much as I contemned the man, and contented myſelf with having done my duty to him.

Mean time I failed not in my enquiries about
you and Gonſalvo, the recollection of whom
conſtantly overcaſt even my happieſt moments, as
the frequent paſſing clouds preparatory to a ſtorm
darken the fair face of day. From the ſtrange
variety of contradictory accounts I received of you
both, I had nothing left to conclude, but that you
had both fallen victims to the rage or jealouſy of the
tyrant; and I never could get rid of a goading
reflection, that by poſſibility I might by my deſer-
tion have excited the monſter's jealouſy and contributed to your ruin.

As I had proved myſelf the zealous adherent
and faithful ſervant of Henry, ſo he proved the
moſt noble and generous of maſters to me.
When by killing the tyrant he got poſſeſſion of
the throne, one of his firſt acts was to beſtow this
eſtate upon me. He ſolicited me earneſtly to remain about his perſon; but on my declaring to
him the ſtate of my mind, and that othing but
the duty I felt to attend him in his dangers could
have ſo long kept me from my ſo much deſired
retirement,

retirement, he gave up the point, and honoured me by faying, How few, Don Ifidor, are
found like you, ready to fhare in a monarch's
dangers, and unwilling to participate of the fplen-
dours of his court! Go, then, you know my
power, be not diftruftful of my inclination—your
fervices exceed the one, but not the other—tax
both to the utmoft, and you fhall not be difappointed: one promife only I exact from you,
namely, that I fee you once a year at leaft.

He has ever fince continued to load me with
favours, and defigns to provide amply for his fon,
for fo he calls Alphonfo. I was performing my
promife of an annual vifit when you firft arrived
here; and I ftill find him the fame generous friend,
the fame gracious and beneficent prince. One of
his chief favourites is married to an aunt of my
wife, the fifter of her father; fhe affects friendfhip, but I can fee that he and fhe abhor me, as
they conceive me to ftand between them and the
inheritance of Don Pedro Guzman, my father-
in-law's eftate: but it is no matter—I know the
king, and have no other feeling for them and
their hatred than contempt.

Since I came here my chief prop has been
my fon Alphonfo; his inftruction has engroffed my
whole care; my daughter being with the Marchionefs

chionefs del Oro in Lifbon, who infifted on tak-.
ing her to herfelf. I muft confefs, that the growing perfections of. my fon,. every day difclofing.
fome new beauty, beguile me of a portion of my
forrows. 'The clouds of mifery that fo entirely
obfcured my happinefs begin to difperfe, and the
prefence and converfation of you, my dear revered.
patron and father (feizing the Baron by the hand),
will help to clear the whole hemifphere before
me, and give the fetting of my life that brightnefs
which your counfel and protection afforded to its
rifing.

One thing now on the expreffions which have
fallen from you about my fon. When I confider
the ftrong refemblance he bears to Gonfalvo,
which I have often with pleafure noted, and which,
confidering their clofe confanguinity, is not fo
very furprifing, coupled with the circumftance of
his bearing the name of Alphonfo, which you fay
was that of Gonfalvo's fon—I cannot fo much
wonder at your emotions : Neverthelefs one thing
has ftruck me with aftonifhment, that a foul fo
vigorous as yours, a mind fraught with all knowledge, and endued with fo much wifdom, could
yield to the fuggeftions of a dream—a creature of
the fancy—a mere being of the imagination :—to
act by the monitions of fuch illufive fhadows, is
to act againft reafon and againft nature.

Nature

Nature, my dear Ifidor, returned the Baron; cannot give us a reafon for all things, as moſt ſceptics expect it ſhould: that phenomenon, the marking of the fœtus by external objects, and even by the workings of the imagination, is as much beyond the reach of human reaſon, as the monitions of a dream or the appearance of departed ſpirits: the difference is, that the experience of almoſt all is in favour of the one, that of few in favour of the other. If, then, we be ſo ignorant of things immediately ſubject to our ſenfes, what muſt we be in thoſe of the ſoul abſtracted from them?

Don Ifidor ſhook his head, but ſaid nothing—Dinner was ſerved in—the happy Alphonſo could hardly eat with the delight the Baron's company afforded him; ſuch charms has cheerful accommodating old age for the tender heart of youth.

It was that day determined, that Don Ifidor ſhould proceed to court, to get the attainder taken off the Baron; and that, till that was effected, he ſhould remain undiſcovered.

G   CHAP.

CHAP. V.

WHEN Alphonſo withdrew after dinner, he was accoſted by Pierrot with, Don Alphonſo—accompanied by a ſignificant wink and beck of his hand, as who ſhould ſay, Follow me—I have ſomething to communicate to you. Alphonſo followed—Pierrot led him through the yard—then looking about to ſee if the place was ſufficiently ſecure from obſervation, he led him into the garden; thence again, with the ſame precaution, into the vineyard, and thence into the field of exerciſe; then leading him into the very middle, as remote as poſſible from any place of concealment where liſteners might ſtand, leſt poſſibly ſome perſon might be there to hear what he was about to ſay— ! taking Alphonſo by a button, and ſtaring full in his face, with a look of infinite ſagacity and importance, he ſaid in a whiſpering voice, Don Alphonſo, do you know this old harper in the great hall? How ſhould I know, Pierrot? ſaid Alphonſo. Does my maſter, Don Iſidor, know him? —Alphonſo, unwilling to break the ſecrecy impoſed

upon

upon him by his father, yet averfe to telling a direct falfehood, replied, How fhould my father know him, fince he has not feen him many hours? I will tell you what it is, mafter——but to be fure it may be a filly thing I am going to fay— No matter, returned the youth, fay it, whatever it may be. Well, then, to be fure, I may be wrong—but my mind mifgives me ftrangely.— What would you fay? Don't fear—I fhall never mention it, fpeak out. As I hope for mercy, the fight of the old harper made my hair ftand on end; nay, the thought of him now makes my blood run in my body, and I wifh he was well away from the houfe. Why, what doft thou mean?. faid Alphonfo. I mean that—but—well I don't know how to fay it. Say it, be what it may, returned Alphonfo. Well, your honour has often heard Don Ifidor talk of the Baron de Rayo—he was a good man to be fure, but that is no matter—I don't like to have any thing to do with the dead! Well, you muft know that this Baron within—I—I mean he that's like him—he, I fay, was in the tower of Siguenca for high treafon —put there by that villain Peter ; and there he died, or, as fome fay, was put to death, by the orders of that devil in grain, whom Chrift pardon!—Don Ifidor took on fo about him, and ufed to figh and

G 2   groan

groan for him; and no wonder, for he was a father to him. Well, what do you think?—but—
but—but—I know you will laugh at me. Indeed,
Pierrot, I will not, let it be what it will I fhall
not laugh at you. Look you, Don Alphonfo,
faid he, clapping one hand on the top of his head,
and the other under his chin, is this head I hold
in my hands, mine or not? Certainly it is, Pierrot.
Then, as fure as it is, the old harper in the hall is
the ghoft of the Baron Rayo, who died in the
tower of Siguenca—it is at leaft his fetch! Body
o' me! I knew him all the time he was at
dinner, in fpite of all his care to hide himfelf;
and I trembled and fhook like an afpen leaf, for he
fpoke in the fame grand way he was wont to
do at Montalto caftle. Lord! your honour's father, who does not fear the devil himfelf (St.
John be our guard!) was as much afraid of the Baron as a moufe of a cat—he was fo grand; and it
furprifes me that Don Ifidor does not know him,
for all his coarfe great coat, leathern belt, and
long beard; but to be fure he is blinded by fome
charm. For my part, I know not what to do—
I am afraid to tell Don Ifidor, and I am afraid
to let him remain unknown in the houfe, for God
and his Holinefs the Pope alone can tell what his
defigns may be—and though he was dearly fond

of

of mafter, when alive, who knows how the other world may turn his heart!

Pierrot, faid Alphonfo, keep this fecret entirely to yourfelf; on no any account, let it go further: I will go in and take proper means to find all out, and let you know—mean time, be fecret, I charge you.

Never fear, your honour: the world fhould not prevail on me to fpeak a word about it contrary to your orders; but, for the bleffed Virgin's fake let Don Ifidor know foon, for I fear there is fome ruination in the old Baron's coming about the houfe.

Alphonfo immediately flew into Don Ifidor's clofet, to difclofe to him and the Baron the converfation between him and Pierrot; and in order to make them more cheerful, he told them the whole as it paffed, but in a manner fo pleafant and humorous, that they both, for the firft time, relaxed into mirth, and gave way to a violent fit of laughter.

The Baron recollected the name of Pierrot, when Don Ifidor mentioned him in his ftory; but as he was fince advanced into years, he did not notice him when attending at dinner. It was agreed however to undeceive him with regard to the Baron's death—to let him know the truth, and

G 3

bind

bind him down to fecrecy. For this purpofe he was called into the clofet: as foon as he entered, the Baron advanced towards him, and with a deep and tremendous tone faid to him, Friend, this youth informs me—Here Pierrot ftood transfixed with horror—his face pale, his noftrils dilated, his eyebrows raifed, and every other mark of a violent agony of fear upon him.—With much difficulty the Baron preferved gravity enough to proceed—Doft thou know ought of me?—Speak. Ye—ye—yes.——That is, N—n—no——Speak, and fear not. Ah, Don Alphonfo! faid Pierrot, with a tremulous voice, I did not think you would —Speak! faid the Baron again, with a voice that fhook the room. Yes, yes, your honour, faid Pierrot, haftily—I did fay to Don Alphonfo, as how I thought that your worfhip was—was— fomething—that is a little like the deceafed wor- thy Baron de Rayo.—Here the Baron took his hand, which he, his mouth yawning wide with excefs of horror, endeavoured to withdraw, and preffing it gently, faid, And why not the Baron himfelf, Pierrot? Has age and this coat fo en- tirely difguifed me that you thought me only a little like Baron de Rayo? Your honour, then, faid Pierrot, brightening, is not dead? Certainly not, faid the Baron. Don Alphonfo! faid Pierrot, did

did not I tell you a month ago, that there was to
be luck in the way; and that I dreamed of a coffin flying, with black wings, over a gallows—a
fure fign, as your worfhip knows, of good. But
you are not dead? No, indeed, faid the Baron
laughing. Then, faid Pierrot, dropping on his
knees, may God keep you fo! It is true, I told
Don Alphonfo, that your fetch was here, but
then I thought your honour was dead—and fo—
and fo your worfhip knows that if you were
dead, you could not be here alive—and fo I was
not fo much to blame: but troth, your honour,
I was hugely frightened; although I am fure,
though I fay it, I would not turn my back upon
e'er a he in the kingdom, excepting your honour,
in fair living fight—but for the dead, I always
abhorred to have any thing to do with them.
Well, then, faid Don Ifidor, you now know the
Baron to be living, and have no further caufe for
fear; fo make it your bufinefs to fee that he is
properly attended, and ferved with the refpect fuitable to his dignity. But, mark me; let not, on
thy peril, a fingle tittle of this difcovery tran-
fpire.

I fhall carefully obey your honour, faid
Pierrot.

It is very true, faid Don Ifidor as Pierrot re-

tired,

tired, a braver fellow, when oppofed to men, never exifted; but he is fuperftitious to an excefs: often has he peftered, indeed oftner diverted me with his dreams; but the very mentioning of the dead feems to fcare him. This is an unaccountable phenomenon in the human heart.

Not at all, returned the Baron; he fears not men, becaufe his fenfes are competent to judge of the danger, and apportion the power of refiftance to it; in which cafe a boldnefs of nature gives him confidence, and makes him eftimate his own prowefs at the higheft: but, in the cafe of fpirits, his foul inftinctively confeffes the exiftence of fuch beings, from falfe conception, or early habit; attributes to them mifchievous difpofitions; while, being out of the compafs of his fenfe, he cannot eftimate their power, and therefore fears them. Thus, however contradictory it may appear to you, it appears perfectly intelligible and natural to me.

Next morning Alphonfo, paffing at an early hour through the armoury, perceived Pierrot hard at work: he had taken down the armour, and was cleaning them with all imaginable induftry.

What is all this for, Pierrot? faid Alphonfo—by whofe directions is it that you take fo much trouble?

trouble? Pierrot looking up in his face, with a countenance full of fagacity and felf-importance, faid, We fhall have rare doings, now that the Baron de Rayo is here—he will be for tilting with you, as he was wont with Don Ifidor and young Henrico Gonfalvo: but tell me, Señor, does the Baron give any account of that fweet young gentleman? Oh, he was the flower of the country! the clevereft, the handfomeft—why, he was almoft as big as the Baron.—Often, often, when I look at you, I think of him, for you are the picture of him; and fo Don Ifidor fays. Ah! Lord help us—where is he now—have you heard, Señor?

No, Pierrot, I have not; not a word. But why this armour?—

Why there would be Don Henrico, and your father, juft when about your age, nay before that, tilting, and lancing, and mock-fighting, perpetually at it, and the Baron looking on and inftructing them: and now you fhall fee—I will wager my head againft a trufs of hay, that before to-morrow night you will fee this armour employed; nay the old Baron himfelf will be at it; but here is no armour to fit him. Alack, Pierrot, he is old. Lord blefs your honour, you little know what tough ftuff the old codger is made of; I'll fuffer

our

our cook to cut off my middle finger and make a
pafty of it, if I would not rather face any three
men in our parifh than him, old as he is; only
make him angry——why it was he that made
Don Ifidor what he was, and fure enough it was
like mafter like fcholar between them, for your
father would fight the devil himfelf: there, at Algeziras, he cut his way through a hundred Moors,
and brought intelligence to the king that faved our
whole army from being cut off by the Infidels—
the king made a knight of him for it. I can't
tell you the particulars of it; for if ever I talked
of it as we rode together, he would ftop me, and
blufh as if he was afhamed of it.

Well, Pïerrot, interrupted Alphonfo, I fhould
not like to hurt any one, but methinks war muft
be glorious fport—fo grand—trumpets founding—
horfes neighing—arms clafhing—the king ap-
plauding.—Oh God! Oh God! it muft be delightful!—Where did you collect all thofe ideas,
my dear, dear boy, faid the Baron, appearing
fuddenly, for furely you fpeak as feelingly, and as
pertinently too, as if you had been already engaged. I have read of them, Sir, returned Alphonfo, and I think I fhould like to try them.—
And try them thou fhalt, my love, faid the Baron,
embracing him.

I wifh

I wifh the Baron may not have overheard me, thought Pierrot to himfelf, recollecting his expreffion of, Old Codger.

Should you like me for a mafter, my dear? faid the Baron.

Indeed I fhould, Sir; but I wifh you a better office. It would ill fuit you to beftow your time on a boy like me.

My dear, rejoined the Baron, your father has configned you entirely to my care, and in doing fo, has conferred on me the greateft poffible favour. All my life ufed to arms, they will, in old age, be my beft paftime; and perhaps it may not be unpleafant to you to hear, that he who was your father's inftructor in arms will be yours. This day then we begin; and, with fo promifing a pupil, I have no doubt of doing every thing.

That I will warrant you, old fellow, faid Pierrot, as the Baron and Alphonfo retired; if fighting will do, you will give him enough of it.— By St. John of God! I believe the Baron thinks that the Almighty made man for no other purpofe but fighting.—God have mercy on his old foul! I am fure it is time for him to think of fomething elfe—but I verily believe thofe fighting people think they are never to die, or that they have no

foul

foul to be faved—With which words Pierrot retired from the armoury, marking his forehead
with a thoufand croffes, and muttering as many
pious ejaculations to the Virgin Mary.

In a few weeks after, Don Ifidor, according to
a plan laid by him, the Baron and Father Thomas, fet off to court, got the attainder of the Baron reverfed, and had fpecial meffengers fent all
over the kingdom, with letters from the gentry at
court, and orders from the king to the magiftrates
of the different towns, to fearch for Gonfalvo, his
wife, and his child : by the king's defire too, the
Archbifhop of Toledo fent difpatches to all the
heads of the church throughout the country to the
fame effect. Thus the Baron was able again to
reaffume his proper appearance ; and had the confolation to think that if his children were living
there was a great probability of their being found,
and to conceive a lively hope that he fhould yet
prefs his grandfon to his bofom.

C H A P.

C H A P. VI.

THE Baron was furprifed to find that his pupil
had already acquired a confiderable fhare of fkill
in the fcience of defence, and that he was an excellent horfeman. His bulk and ftrength too
were prodigious confidering his age, and the
Baron had reafon to believe that he would one
day ride foremoft in the ring of heroes. In a
few months Don Ifidor was prevailed upon to
cafe himfelf in armour, and enter the lifts in mock
fight with his fon: Alphonfo rapidly gained
ground, and, before the end of the fecond year,
Don Ifidor pronounced him to the Baron to be
more than his equal in the encounter. His ftature had enlarged to a fize far above his father's;
the puerile foftnefs of his face began to harden
into the firm features of manhood—the rude bulk
of his limbs to form into the moft perfect fymmetry, and the tender treble of his voice to increafe
into a ftrong manly tenor—The heart of Don
Ifidor expanded with joy, and raifed him almoft
above mortality; while the pride and exultation of

6   the

the Baron fparkled in his eyes, and gave new
vigour and vivacity to his actions—If, faid he
pleafantly one day to Don Ifidor, if I continue
to grow young apace, as I have done fince I came
to your caftle, I fhall be juft of a proper age to
go forth as Alphonfo's fquire at the time that he
will be fit to enter upon the world.

The fharpeft afflictions find a period at laft,
either in death or habit—Thus it was with thofe
of the Baron, who, though the meffengers returned
without being able to get the flighteft trace of
intelligence of his children, began to grow lefs
wretched than he was : he found in Alphonfo
fomething on which to beftow his affection and
employ his time, and the impreffion of his woes
began to be infenfibly effaced from his heart.

The time when Alphonfo fhould make his
appearance on the theatre of life was approaching
faft ; and as the firft ftep was of the utmoft importance, the Baron, Don Ifidor, and Father
Thomas held frequent conferences on the fubject ;
but all their firft plans were rendered abortive,
and Don Ifidor's happinefs interrupted by an event
as lamentable as it was unexpected. King Henry
was fuddenly cut off by poifon, adminiftered by
the intrigues and jealoufy of the Moorifh king of
Granada.

On

On the acceffion of John the fon of Henry to the throne, Don Ifidor went to pay him homage, was received as the friend of his father with diftinction, and found the lofs he fuftained in the late king's death in fome meafure fupplied by the young king's choice of a minifter and favourite, who was Don Juan de Padilla, a moft particular and hearty friend of his. He therefore returned home more affured than he expected, and determined to fend Alphonfo to court, recommended to Don Juan, as foon as poffible, in order that he might be among the firft who offered themfelves as candidates for the favour of the young monarch. He accordingly fet out with all the appointments fuitable to his views, attended by the trufty Pierrot. On his arrival at Burgos, he delivered a letter from his father to Don Juan, who received him with marks of affection and efteem, affured him of his patronage and protection, and told him that he would take a proper opportunity to prefent him to the king.

Don Juan was as good, as his word. Sending one morning for Alphonfo to come to him, he faid, " The king has at my requeft permitted me to prefent you to him, and has appointed this day for the purpofe: he is young, of a charming temper, and moft excellent difpofition ; he is already prepoffeffed

poffeffed in your favour by gratitude for your father's fervices to the late king, you will find little difficulty therefore in making yourfelf agreeable to him."—They went accordingly to the royal chamber, and were admitted to the young monarch; who, after a long converfation with Alphonfo, and after having attentively examined his external deportment as well as his underftanding, turned to Don Juan and faid, "Don Juan de Padilla, of all the young cavaliers whom you have hitherto introduced to me, this is he who fills up in my mind the moft perfect idea of the true gallant cavalier; his perfon is fuperior to any I have feen, and his converfation is a happy mixture of vivacity and good fenfe. Let him be near our perfon as much as is confiftent with his honour and convenience.

The early part of John's reign afforded the young Alphonfo ample occafion to difplay his military talents:—in various encounters with the forces of Portugal, he carried victory along with him in almoft every engagement. And on the defertion of one of John's chief confidential officers, whofe intelligence and knowledge of the Caftilian army's fituation might have given a decided advantage to the enemy, he purfued him to the hoftile army, broke through a large body

of

of them who furrounded the fugitive, feized him, and bore him through them triumphantly on his faddle, back to the Caftilian camp: when this prodigy of valour and prowefs was announced to the king, he exprefled his fatisfaction in the moft lively terms, and feemed to triumph not a little in his forefight and penetration, in having at once discovered in Alphonfo that fuperior heroifm of which he had juft given fo ftriking a fpecimen.

Peace being again reftored, Alphonfo became the conftant companion of the king, from whom he received many flattering marks of favour, and, among others, knighthood.

Among thofe youths of rank who kept about his perfon, and laid claim to his favour, was Don Rodrigo de Calvados, the fon of a deceafed nobleman, a favourite of the late king and of Donna Maria de Guzman, fifter to Don Pedro Guzman, Don Ifidor's father-in-law. By the addrefs and intriguing difpofition of his mother, he had been kept about the court fince his father's death—He was in his nature fubtle, pliant, fawning, and plaufible; with thofe qualities he had contrived to engrofs much of the king's friendfhip to himfelf, till Alphonfo ftepped in, and almoft without an effort engaged a fhare of it. Stung to the quick at the progrefs Alphonfo made in the king's affections, and

H   burning

burning with envy of his superior accomplish-
ments, he conceived the most implacable hatred
against him, and wished for nothing so much
as the destruction of his new rival: his chagrin
became visible; his mother questioned him upon it,
and he hesitated not to tell her the cause. The
ambitious spirit of the lady could ill brook even
a partial suspension of her views in favour of her
son; her soul was up in arms, and her jealousy
was as great of Alphonso's rising favour at court,
as at the prospect he had of inheriting the estate
of his grandfather and her brother Don Pedro
Guzman—The prowess of the youth made an
open quarrel too dangerous an experiment; and
surrounded as they were with crowds of spies, a
plan of treachery was likely to be attended with
equal danger, while his irreproachable conduct
left nothing on which malice itself could ground
an accusation—Thus puzzled, they knew not
what to do, though they agreed that something
must be done.

It was a custom with the king to make parties
of hunting, in which the ladies and gentlemen of
the court attended him; on such occasions they
generally entered a great way into the depths of
the forests, where game was most plenty, and
there pitched tents for their accommodation. As
it

it was now the feason, the king ordered preparations to be made, invited a number of the gentry to attend him, and among the reft Alphonfo, Don Rodrigo and his mother. On the firft day of hunting a large boar was ftarted, which the king purfued, and overtaking, was furioufly affaulted by the animal; by fome mifmanagement of his horfe the king's fpear miffed the boar, who turning fhort, with a rip of his tufk gored the horfe, which fell; and the boar was juft repeating the blow at the king when Alphonfo ftepped in between them, but in fuch a hurry that, inftead of piercing him through the breaft, he only opened a flanting wound in his neck, which rendered him more furious. The king mean-time had difengaged himfelf: Alphonfo, by a fudden and extraordinary fpring, got from the boar before he could make another effort, and meeting him with his fpear killed him on the fpot. All this time Don Rodrigo ftood at a cautious diftance, complimenting the king on his fortunate efcape. As foon as the company came up every mouth was open at once, congratulating his majefty on the fortunate iffue of the affair, who on his part took Alphonfo by the hand, and addreffing the company faid, If my efcape be an event from which you have derived any fatisfaction, join me in gratitude to him whofe gal-

lantry

lantly has, under God, effected it.—Alphonso was fo overwhelmed with the compliments which were lavifhed upon him by all the company, that he could fcarcely bear it: the goodnefs of his monarch was a weight too great. With difficulty he anfwered, If hazarding fo worthlefs a thing as the life of Alphonfo, to fave that on which the glory and happinefs of a nation depend, lays any claim to merit, I am overpaid by the fuccefs of the attempt: do not then heap on me a weight I cannot fupport, by thanking me for doing that which was my duty. ‘God forbid, faid the king, that we fhould fet fo little value on the fervices you have rendered us, as your modefty would have us do! No, Alphonfo, the gratitude of a king would be but poorly fhewn by mere profeffions—your fervices fhall neither be unrewarded nor forgotten.

Although Rodrigo and his mother were among the loudeft in complimenting the youth, the new progrefs he had made by his heroifm, in the heart of the king, was like poifon to their entrails—but when the ladies all expreffed their admiration of his courage, beauty, vigour, and perfon, and above all the modeft dignity with which he received their praifes, the malignant pair could fcarcely reftrain themfelves; nor could Alphonfo,

had

had he known of their evil intentions, have wifhed them a greater curfe than the company of their
own feelings.

What is there which a wicked woman will not
do ? The averfion of Donna Maria de Calvados,
which, but for this late triumph, might have
remained fmothered, now blazed with ten-fold
fury : fhe riveted her eyes on him, and fecretly
wifhed that they had the power of thofe of the
bafilifk, that fhe might look him dead. As fhe
looked at him, fhe thought fhe beheld features that
fhe had once been acquainted with.

This worthy lady had, previous to her marriage
with Don Rodrigo's father, feen and conceived a
tendernefs for Gonfalvo, when he was firft brought
to court : nay, fhe had made overtures to him, of
which his attachment to the daughter of the Baron
de Rayo would not permit him to take advantage. It is no wonder then if the refemblance
which Alphonfo de Haro bore to that Gonfalvo
fhould be foon recognifed. She was aftonifhed
at it; fhe thought it beyond the ufual courfe of
nature ; and meafuring her belief by her wifhes
rather than by the facts, fhe fet it down that he
was really his fon, and upon that fuggeftion,
idle though it was, formed a plan, which fhe determined to put in immediate execution. She

H 3   informed

informed her fon of her fufpicions, on which fhe
faid that fhe was refolved to act as if on certainty, and charged him to co-operate with her
in informing the king. To this Rodrigo objected,
that his doing fo might raife fufpicions in the mind
of John, for that he was fo attached to Alphonfo,
nothing lefs than pofitive evidence could fhake him
in his favour.

The mother aware of this circumftance, as well
as her fon, now thought that an anonymous letter
would be the beft and fafeft way to try the temper
of the king on the bufinefs. They fat down together therefore and produced the following letter,
which Rodrigo contrived to have dropped in the
king's private clofet.

" Moft gracious fovereign,

" When treafon lurks in any fhape about your
majefty's throne, it is the duty of every fubject
to apprize you of the danger.

" A fon of that traitor to the crown of Caftile,
the fugitive Henrico Gonfalvo, is now, under the
falfe name of De Haro, near your facred perfon:
the old viper has eluded juftice—crufh the young
one ere it fting you."

As foon as the king received this letter, his
efteem for Alphonfo directly fuggefted to him
the truth, that it was the work of fome envious
enemy;

enemy; he therefore fent for Don Juan de Padilla, and, firft fhewing him the letter, told him his fentiments of it.

Were not this artifice, faid Don Juan, too fhallow for the genius of Donna Maria de Calvados, I fhould fufpect her of being at the head of it; her whole life has been one continued fcene of court intrigue, and fhe is moft likely to be jealous of the favours you lavifh on this young man in preference to her fon, without confidering the great difference in their talents and qualifications. As it is only juftice to the youth, however, that the mafk fhould be torn from the face of his enemies, I fhall take the liberty of fuggefting to your majefty a mode that cannot fail of difcovering them.

The young king, highly pleafed, faid he would join in it moft willingly, and defired him to propofe it.

Order Alphonfo to withdraw from court, faid Don Juan.

Order Alphonfo to depart from court! interrupted the king.

May it pleafe your majefty to hear me—The intrigues of your majefty's enemies in the court of Portugal require obfervation, and we have already

agreed to retain fome noble and faithful Caſti-
lians privately in your fervice there : let Alphonfo,
under a feigned name, proceed thither among the
reſt, while I make it known that he is difmiſſed in
confequence of this private admonition.

And what end will this anfwer? demanded the
king, who did not reliſh the parting with Alphonfo.

Your majeſty ſhall know, returned Don Juan.
When he is gone, your majeſty may exprefs a defire to know to whofe fidelity and good offices
you are indebted for the admonitory letter, and
doubt not but that, eager for perfonal approbation,
they will difclofe themfelves.

- The king immediately fell in with the plan of
Don Juan, who fent for Alphonfo, told him the
affair exaƈtly as it was, opened to him the plan,
and concluded with telling him that it offered an
opportunity of feeing Lifbon, which would not
only amufe him, but contribute to his information
and improvement.

- Alphonfo appearing much concerned, Don Juan
earneſtly enquired if the plan was difagreeable to
him.

Oh, no, no, Señor ! replied Alphonfo ; but I am
ſtung to the foul to think that I ſhould have de-

ported

ported myself so as to make an enemy: but, alas!
this is but a small concern; the thought of giving trouble to my sovereign afflicts me most:
what am I, that so good, so great; so august a
monarch should throw away a thought upon me?
and what but injury can it be to me to discover
who my enemies are, since I must necessarily revenge myself or despise them?

Noble youth, said Don Juan, you are irresist-
ible—yours are the sentiments of true nobility; I
almost wish I could indulge you: but the king
has made the affair his own, and will not be
contradicted.

Little preparation was necessary for Alphonso: the king sent for him, took him into his
closet, shewed him the letter, assured him of his
eternal friendship, and told him that he expected
his return as soon as he should signify his desire
for it; which would happen when a proper disco-
very took place, or when it was despaired of.—
Alphonso threw himself at the king's feet, kissed
his hand, and bathed it with tears of gratitude:
May no disloyalty or disaffection, but such as
mine, said he, ever approach your sacred throne!
The king then presenting him a paper to be delivered to Don Juan, and putting a costly ring
upon his finger, bid him adieu.

He

He waited on Don Juan immediately; who reading the paper, told him that it was an order to pay him two thoufand piaftres for the expences of his journey.

That night Alphonfo, attended by Pierrot and two guides, fet out for Portugal; and the next day it was whifpered that the king had difmiffed him in difgrace. From the firft town he went he wrote a letter to his father, and another to the Baron, informing them of the recent event, and defiring a letter to his aunt, the countefs of Leiria, in Lifbon.

At the end of three days the guides left them, and he and Pierrot were left to themfelves: the latter, who was by nature fociable and loquacious, thinking the departure of the guides gave him a licenfe to converfe with his mafter, afked him whither and for what end he was going?

I am going, Pierrot, faid the youth, to fee tha grand and univerfally admired city Lifbon, and to fearch for adventures as a valiant Chriftian knight fhould do.

I do not underftand what your honour means by adventures.

I am going then, faid he, to redrefs grievances, to right wrongs, to protect, when it falls in my way, poverty and weaknefs, againft the violence and

and encroachments of the wealthy, the proud, and the ſtrong.

God and the bleſſed Virgin proſper ſuch intentions! To help the weak and the poor is good; but I doubt me your honour is too ready to fight for the ſtrong and the great too. Now, although fighting be a very good thing upon occaſions, when one is obliged to do it (and I can myſelf take and give a few hard knocks, as the ſaying is, when need requires, as well as another), yet methinks it is a ſtrange ſort of a trade to follow, and very unfit for a gentleman above all others.

Why for a gentleman, Pierrot? ſaid Alphonſo, who liked his diſcourſe.

I'll tell your honour—When a poor fellow is reduced to get his bread by knocking others in the head, it is hard enough upon him, but ſtill perhaps he can do no better; and if he endures hardſhip, or is knocked in the head himſelf, he may comfort himſelf with the thoughts that he might have endured worſe;—but here is your honour, who might be comfortable and warm at home, ſet out on a wild-gooſe chace to look for fighting, and after getting enough to ſatisfy a reaſonable appetite on the part of the king, are
now

now going, for lack of better, to look for more of it on the part of the beggars.

But, Pierrot, honour is as great a reward, and as neceffary to the exiftence of a gentleman, as bread is to that of the peafant.

I fhould be glad to know, returned Pierrot, what honour there can be in breaking bones, cracking of crowns, or poking fpears into men's guts. I think it would be more honour to be fitting at home with your father, or playing innocently with the old armour, and the fierce old Baron at home at the caftle of Duero.

But, Pierrot, faid the youth, if fome of us did not fight, we fhould become a prey to our enemies, and to all bad men who chofe to wrong us.

Time enough, I fay, ftill, when it comes to one's hand; but why run our heads againft ftonewalls, as the faying is? Your honour's father was as brave a warrior as any in Spain; but he was wife enough at laft to go and ftay at home in peace; and he has done more good, and got more honour in one week fince, than he could have got in fifty years mad prize-fighting about the world. There is the old Baron de Rayo—why I fuppofe he has fought more than a thoufand tigers, and

what

what is he the better for it? What was his honour at laft? Why, an old baize coat, and a tune
on the harp for his dinner. There was the noble
Henrico Gonfalvo—he took a flight after honour,
as you call it, and never came back again. Mark
me, dear mafter, I am old, and can inftruct from
experience, more than others from books—honour
is a very dangerous flippery thing—it is like a ghoft
—you think you fee it—you may catch at it, but
you never can hold it faft; and for my part, I
have feen fo much ruination brought about you
all by it, that I tremble at the name, almoft as much
as I do at that of a ghoft!

Upon my word, Pierrot, I had no conception
that you were fo ingenious a cafuift—Proceed,
for notwithftanding your erroneous imagination,
your argument pleafes me.

Well, then, your honour, there's Don—Don—
Diabolo! oh, Don Rodrigo; he, too, is one of
your men of honour. It feems then, honour is
got different ways; for the day you took a fancy
to try how a wild boar's tufk felt, and ran fo honourably between death and the king, Don Rodrigo fhook from head to foot—I was near him—
his face was the picture of death—and I plainly
perceived other marks of fear, which I won't
mention.—Well, this Don Rodrigo is a man of

honour

honour too—Now the queftion is this, If honour be got by cowardice, is it worth the labour and danger of fighting for?

Pierrot, faid Alphonfo, with all your fimplicity you have put a queftion now that would puzzle a learned clerk to expound; but ftill from miftaking the fubject. If, as you fay, Don Rodrigo be a coward (which I believe is only the effect of your imagination), it muft be confidered as a misfortune, not a difhonour: it is true, he is in that cafe, not a man of military honour—but he may be a man of moral honour; and being a favourite of the king, the prefumption is, that he muft be in fome refpects honourable. For, know, Pierrot, that the roads to the temple of honour are many; and it is of little confequence which a man takes, fo he purfues that for which he is qualified by nature, and makes true religion his guide, and a clear confcience his companion.

Now, your honour, quoth Pierrot, hath tied a knot with your tongue which you cannot untie with your teeth, though they were each as ftrong as that faid boar's tufks,—You fay honour is your aim—Very well—There are many roads, you fay, to honour, no matter which you take—Then why not take the plain, eafy, comfortable path, home? There, with your father and your friends, by and

by

by with a pretty wife and a parcel of children, blessing all the poor with your bounty, they blessing you with their prayers—ah, Señor, there would be honour, there would be glory—But this pate-breaking, bloody, cut and thrust work—a plague upon it! I say—it is inhuman, unchristian, and abominable; and I cannot abide the thoughts of it, unless, as I said before, it falls in one's way, and then I will make the best use of the arms God gave me, and defend myself.

It was evening when this conversation passed between Alphonso and his faithful servant Pierrot. Just as the latter had concluded his last sentence, they were suddenly alarmed with the screaming of female voices at some distance before them in the forest—Alphonso, who, by the interruption of the trees, could not see the objects from whom the noise proceeded, spurred on his courser, and was followed close by Pierrot, whose aversion to fighting was more the result of his reason than the dictates of his heart, and who, in an instant, forgot all his prudent apothegms, and drove on his horse with as great eagerness as ever did knight of chivalry. After riding at full speed a few hundred yards, they found that the object of their pursuit had changed its position, and that the screams were more to the right hand, and observ-

ed

ed that they were growing fainter, while the trampling of horfes plainly befpoke a flight, and convinced him that no time was to be loft. They therefore turned to the right, and preffed forward with all their fpeed: for a confiderable time they followed the noife, fometimes coming nearer, fometimes lofing the found, till at length they observed before them a chaife driving full fpeed, and guarded by a number of men well mounted and armed. At this fight they pufhed their horfes harder; and that which Pierrot rode being fwifter than his mafter's, which was of the larger and heavier kind, he got up firft, and concluding how things were, rufhed eagerly by the horfemen, and with a ftroke levelled the driver of the chaife, and then with a dextrous blow gave one of the mules which drew it a cut on the back of the neck, which laid him dead, and effectually ftopped the progrefs of the whole; then turning about upon the horfemen, who had been already charged by Alphonfo, they both laid about them with fuch fury, that after laying one dead, and wounding three others fo that they could not efcape, they put the remainder to flight. Alphonfo then came up to the chaife, and found in it two ladies, one of whom had fainted, and was fupported by the other, who demonftrated every mark of difmay and diftraction. The

veil

veil of the lady who fainted was kept carefully
down by the other; which Alphonso perceiving
said, It is my earneft wifh, lady, to render you
and your companion who has fainted, every affiftance in my power; but I fear my prefence
may, for fome reafons, be at this time improper.
I fhall, if that be the cafe, withdraw, and ftand
within hearing, till it may be your pleafure to call
upon me: meantime, madam, fear nothing; for be
affured, that he who has had the felicity to ftep
between you and the violence intended you, will
protect your perfon to whatever place you may
think it expedient to go for fecurity.

Pardon me, fir, returned the lady, after a paufe,
in which fhe viewed the youth with an earneft
eye, if, in the confternation I was in at the fcene
which has juft paffed, I fhould have confounded
innocence with guilt, and conceived that we had
been faved from one ruffian only to be fubjected to
the violence of another; but as the courtefy of
your expreffions, the delicacy of your manner,
and, let me add, the noblenefs of your air, pro-
claim you incapable of difhonour, I fhall not
fcruple to put myfelf under your protection, and
entreat your affiftance to convey us to a town not
two leagues hence, where I fhall be tolerably fecure till I can profecute my journey: mean time I

fhall

shall be obliged to you to order your servant to bring a drop of water to the relief of this young lady. Alphonso immediately ran off, and in a few minutes returned with some water in his helmet, which he with many apologies presented to the lady; who removing the veil from the face of her who had fainted, discovered to the astonished youth the most exquisitely beautiful set of features he had ever beheld.

But if he thought them beautiful while bespread with the pale hue of death, what were his sensations when, as life returned, expression and colour were restored to her cheeks, and when opening her eyelids she stared wildly around her, and discovered a pair of eyes so far beyond any he had ever beheld! He was lost in rapturous astonishment—while she cried—Oh save me!—save me!—in pity save me from the tyrant!—Alas, where are we?—who is this cavalier? But why do I ask? He is one of the Duke's creatures! Yet surely he looks noble, and wears not the face of a ruffian.—Tell me, dear madam, where are we? —are we safe?—what means this pause of quiet so different from that which passed but now? Compose yourself, my child, said the elder, all is well: the perturbation of your spirits calls for rest; therefore refrain for the present from interrogating me, and content yourself with the assurance that we are safe as yet.

3   Rely,

Rely, ladies, said Alphonso, upon such protection as I and my servant can afford you ; and rest assured that we will still defend you while we have life to move an arm.

It is not a few Portuguese that shall hurt you, said Pierrot, with a bow to the chaise, by way of hint to the ladies to be of good cheer.

I already perceive that, my good friend, said the lady.

Every thing being arranged in the best manner circumstances would allow of, and the prisoners secured, the ladies and their gallant champions set forward towards the town, where they arrived at a late hour. The ladies retired to a chamber, while Alphonso and Pierrot went to a magistrate, who dispatched a guard to bring the wounded men, attended by Pierrot to shew the place.

The ladies and Alphonso supped together—during supper, he sucked in the poison of love in such large draughts that he found little room for food ; while the elder lady cursorily hinted, that she was flying with her young ward into Spain, to release her from the addresses of an importunate amorous old nobleman of Portugal, whose influence at court made it dangerous to offend him. She added, that finding her going, he had taken that violent method of procuring by force that

which

which was denied to his rank, wealth, and folicitations.

Alphonfo paid her a handfome compliment on
the generofity and difintereftednefs of her principles.; faid, that to give fuch youth, innocence,
and beauty to the poffeffion of old age, would be
a crime worfe than facrilege; expreffed his joy
at having been inftrumental to her fafety, although
he forefaw that his peace of mind for ever was the
price at which he had purchafed it; and concluded with a vehement declaration of love.

The elder lady faid, that fhe hoped he would
confine his difcourfe to fuch fubjects as fhe could
liften to—that indebted though they were to his
valour and generofity, their acquaintance was too
fhort, their knowledge of each other too flight,
the paffion he had avowed too fuddenly formed, to
countenance either him in making fuch a declaration, or her in liftening to it. She therefore entreated that he would be filent on that fubject,
elfe fhe fhould be obliged, however unwillingly, to
retire. Alphonfo bowed, and for the reft of the
fhort time they fat together confined himfelf to
the language of the eyes.

Alphonfo flept not the whole night; he toffed,
he tumbled, he fighed; he formed a thoufand
ftrange, vague plans, every one of which he again
rejected:

rejected: at last he determined to discover to the ladies who he was, in order to secure a favourable reception. At day-break he arose, and calling Pierrot, was by him informed, that the ladies, after parting from him, had given orders for the chaise and fresh mules, and departed.

Alphonso was in an agony of despair—he immediately took horse and pursued them in the route towards the confines of Spain, till their horses were unable to proceed, and he found pursuit vain. Alas! said he, what a wretch am I, to have seen such beauty, and to have it snatched from me in an instant!—Ungrateful!—no mark, no proof of gratitude or regard!—Oh God! Oh God! would that I were dead!

As to mark, if you mean a token, said Pierrot, perhaps we have got one without their consent or desire: look at this, said he, producing a small picture of the young and beauteous object of his affection.

Gracious God! exclaimed Alphonso—how—where—by what means did you get this?—did the dear lovely—cruel—did she give it?

No, said Pierrot.

How then? demanded Alphonso.

Why, when the alguazils and I went to the spot where we rescued the ladies, to look for the

I 3 wounded

wounded ruffians, we could not find them; and searching about clofely with the lanterns, I found that picture lying on the ground, which I brought back with a determination to give it to the lady; but now they are gone, I am glad you have it.

Bleffed be your heart, my honeft Pierrot! returned Alphonfo; never fhall this be forgotten to thee: for this, even this, will be fome comfort, fome confolation, under my miferies.

They then turned back towards Portugal by another road, and without further accident reached the city of Lifbon; where, to his great regret, he found that his aunt had, in confequence of the death of her hufband, retired from Lifbon, and gone again into Spain.

CHAP.

CHAP. VII.

IT was now that feason of the year when the people of all Chriftian countries devote themfelves to
joy, feftivity, and thankfgiving, in anniverfary com-
memoration of the birth of the Saviour of mankind,
when Alphonfo fet out from Lifbon on his return
to Caftile, in confequence of a meffage from the
king, who defired him to leave Portugal and return into Spain. He had formed the refolution of
feeing as much as he could of the country, before
his return; and therefore vifited the city of Seville, purpofing thence to proceed to Cordova,
and fo to Burgos. He left Seville on Chriftmas
eve, and had already come near the ancient town
of Carmona, when hearing a more than ufual
noife of bells ringing, he demanded of a fhepherd,
whom he accidentally overtook in the road, what
was the occafion of it? You muft be a ftranger to
Spain, although you fpeak the Caftilian tongue,
faid the fhepherd, not to know that to-morrow

I 4   will

will be the nativity of our blessed Redeemer, and that on this account the bells are ringing. I am, returned Alphonso, a Castilian, and a true Christian, thank God; but a long journey, and a variety of incidents, prevented me from attending to the time: I knew it was the season, but was perfectly heedless of the day itself being so near. Shall I be able to reach Cordova to-night? You may, returned the shepherd, if your horse be able to keep the pace he is at, and you happen to hit the right road, which I assure you is very difficult and very dangerous too; for there be so many roads before you, running like your fingers from your hand, that you will be very apt to miss the true one, and the caverns and old Moorish towers on the ridges of the Sierra Morena, are filled with bands of robbers: however, keep to the right of yonder brow that is topped with a broken rock resembling a tower; as you proceed by that, you will keep still to the right till you come near the town of Palma; keep to the left of it, and you will probably meet some goatherd who can direct you; if not, God and our blessed Virgin be your guide!

As soon as they parted from the shepherd, Alphonso quickened his pace. If I were allowed to advise, said Pierrot, we should proceed to the town of

Palma,

Palma, of which the shepherd spoke, and there go to midnight mass, and on the morrow proceed with a proper guide to Cordova: for it is not alone the robbers of which he told you that we have to dread; but this being the season when the fairies and all forts of goblins are wandering about and playing their frolics, who knows what mischief may befall us?—And if we should chance to be misled by any of those malicious demons, and beguiled into those mountains, which look a thousand times blacker than night itself, we might possibly fall into the bowels of some monstrous cavern, or tumble down some of those frightful precipices with which I am sure those mountains abound.

Pierrot, interrupted Alphonso, why should you, being a Christian, suppose that we have more to fear from demons, as you call them, at this season than at another? I should suppose that we have rather less. However, I am positively determined to proceed; meantime you may remain behind, and follow me at your leisure: your fears might probably produce those very mischiefs of which you express such apprehension; therefore turn you into Palma, while I push on to Cordova. Pierrot said not a word, but followed his master, who pushed forward briskly. Night drew on apace, and

and they infenfibly became fhrouded in the bofom of a deep foreſt, bounded on either fide by ſtupendous mountains, which rifing almoſt perpendicularly hid their heads in the ſkies, and whoſe rugged protuberances feemed to frown with favage afpect on the narrow path that wound through the wood below. The awful folemnity of the fcene was increafed by a rapid rill of water, which growled adown the bofom of a glen, and, burſting into a fudden cataract, thundered on the rock below. Señor, faid Pierrot earneſtly, hear me, for the bleſſed Virgin's fake hear me; remember that a fool's advice has faved many a wife man from ruination. I warn you that we are going aftray—return, for the love of Chriſt, and do not run headlong upon your fate. Peace, peace! returned Alphonfo—didſt thou ever fee a fpot fo calculated to call up ideas of fublimity and magnificence? Didſt thou ever fee fo charming a night? The moon herſelf feems to aſſume increaſed ſplendour, to chafe away the obtruding clouds, and fhine with unobſtructed luſtre on the bufinefs of this night. Bleſſed Virgin! what is that? exclaimed Pierrot. What do you talk of? faid Alphonfo. If I live, faid Pierrot, I faw the ſtrangeſt fight——It is your fear, not your eyes that faw it, returned Alphonfo. Juſt as he fpoke,

he

he defcried a perfon of more than common fize
before him, who feemed walking haftily through
the path of the foreft, in the fame direction that
he was going: he fpurred his horfe into a round
pace in order to come up with him; but, though
he at laft pufhed him to a gallop, the object ftill
kept before him, till coming to an angle formed
by a narrow road, at the foot of a perpendicular
corner of the hill, of immenfe height, he turned
round it, and got out of fight. Alphonfo ftill
quickening his pace, turned it alfo, and found a
vaft open plain, extenfive beyond fight. Nothing
was to be feen—he drew in his bridle, and ftood
bewildered in contemplation, while all was wrap-
ped in a filence truly awful : he was loft in aftonifhment, and remained for fome time in a ftate
of doubt and contemplation. At length turning to
Pierrot, whofe fears were wound up to a pitch of
fuperftitious horror not to be defcribed, It is
not poffible, faid he, that this delicious plain
fhould be uninhabited, yet can I fee no trace of
human refidence, and the moon is fo bright that
I think I fhould if there were any. I will holla
aloud—perhaps there may be fome one within
hearing. He then called out with all his might,
and was anfwered by an echo which reverberated
his

his voice a number of times, increasing each time in loudness till at last it died away in the same number of reverberations again. Utter dismay seized Pierrot—Alphonso was not perfectly at ease—not a soul appeared—he waited many minutes with impatience ——I will holla again, said he.—For the mercy of God, Señor, said Pierrot, take care what you do—let us call upon Heaven, and turn our horses back again into the path we came. Alphonso perceiving no track in the plain before him, agreed to do as Pierrot advised him, and turned towards the road from which he had wandered in pursuit of the figure. He had scarcely gone three steps when the air was filled with lamentable screeches—he stopped —they ceased.—Blessed Virgin! said Pierrot, where are we got, or what can those screeches mean? Sot, cried Alphonso rather peevishly, do you not perceive that they are owls which fly in clouds about us? By this time he again bethought him of the road, and being at the corner looked out for it, and perceived many paths leading through the forest in that direction; While he was considering which of them to take, a sigh of deep anguish, heaved as from the bosom of a giant behind him, caught his ear: he turned his head,

and

and again faw the figure walking at an eafy pace; he wheeled round his horfe and again purfued, obferving it attentively: it had a long fpear in its hand, and glided with amazing fwiftnefs before him. Stop, faid he in a loud voice, ftop, and I fwear by the God of Chriftians you fhall receive no harm. Immediately the vaft concave of the hills was filled all round with an echo, which in the moft awful manner repeated, You fhall receive no harm. The figure outftripped him, and again difappeared. Alphonfo paufed—then turning to Pierrot faid, There muft be fomething in this— come of it what will, I am determined to proceed in this direction and then fpurred his horfe for-ward. He had not gone far, when the moon all at once became obfcured—the moft difmal darknefs, interrupted ever and anon with flafhes of lightning which ferved but to make it the more horrible, fuc-ceeded : rain fell in torrents, while the wind blew as if it would root up the furrounding mountains from their bafes, and filled the air with groans and hollow founds. He fpurred his horfe into a gallop, throwing the reins on his neck, and leaving him to his own direction—or to that of a fuperior guide.

He had not rode long before he found his horfe ftop fuddenly; and looking attentively before him, thought that through the dark void he could per-ceive

ceive a high wall with battlements : he again
called out aloud ; a tumultuous noife was heard,
and all at once he perceived feveral large windows,
refembling thofe of a church illuminated by a
ftrong light from within. Concluding it to be
a chapel lighted up for the purpofe of celebrating
midnight mafs, he bleffed God for the miraculous
event which led him to it, and difmounting from
his horfe fought out an entrance.—There was none
on that end, and the place on either fide was fo clofely inveloped in thick underwood and bufhes, that he
found fome difficulty in getting through them. He
pierced through, however, and found in the fide a
door open ; he entered it, and, paffing through an
aifle perfectly illuminated, found himfelf in the body
of a magnificent church and very near the altar. He
wondered much to find that there was no one in
it ; but concluding that the priefts were in the
facrifty and the congregation not come, he knelt
down to pray. Scarcely had he been in this pofture two minutes, when mufic the moft heavenly
ftruck up, and he heard the De Profundis chanted
by voices more than human, and the whole fabric
fhook with the notes of an organ whofe deep tones
equalled thofe of thunder. He heard, but faw
no one, and was riveted to the ground with aftonifhment—the mufic ftopped—a bell that feemed

to

to fhake the church to its foundation tolled, and he reckoned twelve—the light vanifhed—his ears were affailed with the moſt piercing fighs—a hideous noiſe like the craſhing of a vaſt pile of falling rocks was heard—he drew his fword, and offered up a prayer to Heaven for his fafety—A noiſe, as of the flight of an immenſe pair of wings paffing through the air, was heard wafting its heavy way round the vaulted cieling of the aiſle— The reſolution even of Alphonſo could fcarcely fupport it. Whatever thou art, faid he in a low and folemn tone, that haſt led me into this perilous and awful place, I conjure thee by him whom the Almighty this bleſſed night gave as a ranſom for our fins, to fpeak thy intent.—He pauſed for a reply, while his briſtled hair ſtood erect upon his head, the marrow in his bones froze as into ſtone, and his head even to the deep receſſes of his brain felt as if congealed into ſolid ice. He heard the claſhing of a fword againſt armour—his mind was wrought up to the madneſs of horrid expectation—and ſtraight a figure, ſuch as he had feen, but rendered viſible by a lambent flame which played about it, ſtood before him. It feemed far above the common ſize, but its afpect was rendered ſtill more formidable by an enormous warlike plume that nodded on its helmet,

and

and feemed reflected as in a mirror, in the brightnefs of the armour in which it was cafed. Excefs
of horror wound up the finking fpirits of Alphonfo, and he put himfelf in a firm pofture of
defence—Whatever thou art, faid he, approach
no nearer—my truft is in the Almighty, and if
thou be wicked thou canft not hurt me. If there
be aught that I can do——The figure fighed. Alphonfo's fear was loft in compaffion and curiofity
—Fear not, dear youth, faid the figure, referve your
fword for vengeance.—With thofe words, the
helmet fell from his head, and difclofed a countenance of majeftic fadnefs, pale, bloody; while
long redundant hair entangled with clotted gore
hung in loofe diforder over his fhoulders : again
it fighed, then glided backwards till it reached the
wall, which yawned and fhut him in. Alphonfo,
his fenfes fufpended between amazement and
pity, by a convulfive impulfe of which he was
unconfcious, darted forward, and plunged his
fword after the figure into the wall, which clofing
held it faft.—He exerted all his ftrength to draw it
out, in vain. While he was thus engaged, a ftrain
of mufic more foothing than human fkill could
produce, ftruck up, and lulled him by degrees
into a fweet and gentle fleep, and he funk upon
the ground. The figure ftill was prefent to his

imagination

imagination—he dreamed that it took him by the hand, and, leading him through a number of dark and intricate windings, prefented him to Baron de Rayo, faying, To your conduct I confign him—and then prefenting him a large key faid, Take this, confult the Baron, and be refolute—nor bolts, nor bars, nor walls of adamant, nor human fraud nor human force can refift thofe whom God has defigned to be the inftruments of Heaven's vengeance. On which the armour of the figure gaped, a fkeleton fell from it in fragments at his feet; while the coat clofed upon him, the helmet and plumes lodged upon his head, and he found himfelf armed cap-a-pee: encumbered with the unufual weight he ftruggled and awoke, and perceived that day had dawned.

His firft fenfations on awaking were little more than a dream: he was bewildered in a maze of awe and wonder at what he had feen, and in ftrange conjectures on that which he had dreamed; he could hardly determine at firft, whether the whole had not been a dream, till looking at the wall he perceived his fword fticking in it: he caught it by the hilt, intending to ufe all his ftrength to draw it out, but it yielded to a twitch. In doing this he miffed his ring; he fought for it up and down the floor for fome time in vain:

K

at

at laft recollecting the violence of his efforts in
the night to draw forth his fword, he turned to
fearch there. There was a fmall heap of rubbifh
lying under: he fcraped it up in fearch of the ring,
which he found : juft as he took the ring up, he
perceived a key lying in the rubbifh, and fnatching it up alfo faw that it exactly refembled that
which he had dreamed of.—Gracious God ! he
exclaimed, to what myfterious agency am I thus
conducted ? then kneeling, and devoutly lifting
up his hands and eyes to Heaven, fervently prayed
for fortitude and wifdom proportioned to the
great work of which he faw himfelf likely to
be made the inftrument.

Having thus prayed, he found himfelf unufually
invigorated and cheerful :—he looked around him,
and was furprifed to find the face of every thing
entirely different from that which he had the preceding night conceived it to be. He found that
the church had been fuffered to fall to ruin—
branches of the trees without were ftriking
through the half-demolifhed window-cafes—weeds
were growing near that which had been the
altar—the cieling was pierced with holes and
breaches which ferved as nefts for various birds—
there were no doors but one fmall one which were
not ftopped up. He got up into one of the win-

dows,

dows, and faw a large fpace refembling a garden, but filled with trees, whofe fpreading branches inter-woven with each other almoft excluded light or air, while the bottom was choked with noifome weeds, briers and bufhes : this fpace was bounded on the other fide by a large building, which though very high had no windows in that direc-tion. He again defcended, and went into the aifle, which he found in the fame way inveloped in bufhes; he fought for the door by which he had entered, and with difficulty found it; it was a winding paffage through a wall—a great gate (once the entrance) he obferved to be carefully clofed up, but it was in a different direction from the paffage at which he had come in. He then re-turned to the chapel, and with a fcrutinizing eye obferved the place where his fword was ftuck, in order to mark it : he took out his book and accu-rately noted all the particulars, the altar ferving him as the great guiding mark; then, going out through the aifle and narrow paffage, with diffi-culty made his way through the bufhes, marking it carefully however by breaking down fome large branches. After winding round the wall he found Pierrot waiting in fuch a ftate of horror and fuf-penfe as human nature was fcarcely able to fup-port—Had you ftayed much longer, Señor, faid

he,

he, I fhould have expired—How you have the heart to endure fuch things I cannot tell—I am fure I am afraid of no living man that ever wore a head, and yet if my hair be not turned white with fear I much wonder at it.—Why, what now? what has been the matter?—Matter, your honour! —God knows, matter enough—why, your honour had not gone as long as I could reckon ten, when all the lights in the windows went out—and then I heard a clafhing of fwords—and then groaning —and then fhrieks, like thofe of unfortunate departed fouls in trouble. I thought that the life would leave me: however, fearing you might have been attacked, I refolved not to aét like a cowardly rafcal, and got off my horfe, drew my fword, and went round this wall: then the noife ceafed; I attempted to break through the bufhes, but, oh Lord! if I am here alive, a thoufand fnakes began to hifs at me like red hot horfe-fhoes in water, fo that I was fain in fpite of me to draw back. When I returned to the place where I left the horfes, I found that they had run off about the plain; a plague upon them!—I ran after them, for the moon fhone bright again, and, a curfe confound the brutes! they would not let me catch them till about ten minutes ago. I at laft began to think of going in to look for you, and if I could not find you

2   to

to set off to Don Ifidor as fast as I could, to tell him
the difmal news ; but, thanks to the blefled Virgin!
you are here, and, as I think, fafe. So mount your
horfe, clap fpurs to him, and without once looking
behind you gallop away from this manfion of
demons, fairies, ghofts and devils—Lord, Señor !
are not you dead with fear ? Make hafte, make
hafte ; and when you get out of the way of the
demons—I mean the good people that inhabit this
place—let me know what befel you : but do not
fay a word here ; for they would fet us all wrong
in an inftant, and keep us another night, perhaps
for ever, in this abominable place, which looks
fomehow more black and gloomy than hell itfelf.
Nay, I dare fay, that every ftep we move we tread
on the bodies of murdered people—hafte you
therefore, dear mafter of mine, hafte you—mount
your horfe, and let us be away as faft as our beft
legs can carry us.

Pierrot, faid Alphonfo, I do firmly believe you
to be, in an encounter with mere flefh and blood
like yourfelf, as brave a fellow as ever Caftile bred :
but fuperftition makes you in other cafes a coward to excefs—I fay to excefs, for it deprives you
of your fenfes. What ftronger proof can there be
of this, than your diftafte to this place ? which I
folemnly declare I think to be the moft charming

fpot.

ſpot by far that I have ever beheld: here there is
nothing wanting which can render the face of a
country enchanting.

Aye, aye, interrupted Pierrot, God knows,
there are charms and enchantments enough in
it: but for mercy's ſake, Señor, make haſte, and
let us begone before it grows dark—I dare ſay that
the evening is approaching faſt.

There again, returned the youth, you betray
the madneſs occaſioned by your fears. Why,
ſot, do you not perceive that it is yet ſcarcely
morning? Even now the ſun barely ſprings from
the top of yonder hill, and with feeble rays ſhines
upon us ſo obliquely, that our ſhadows reach almoſt beyond our ſight. I cannot leave this cheering ſpot till I indulge my ſight with more of its
beauties. Methinks I could live here for ever!
Behold how yonder mountain, ſteep, almoſt perpendicular, rears on the ſouth its huge ſtupendous
head to the clouds, and ſhields the plain below
from the ſcorching power of the ſun's meridian
heat—while the earth, as if grateful for its protection, ſpreads at its feet a rich carpet of never-
fading green! Look again to the weſt—ſee where
myriads of oaks and cork trees, ranged by the hand
of nature in gay and beautiful parade, one above
the other, up the ſlope of that hill, ſpread in

kindly

kindly majefty their arms afar, and join to form a canopy unequalled in the palaces of princes, to fhade the fhepherd and his flock from the fultry evening's heat; and fee above them, on the grafly top, the fhepherd now draws forth his flock to feed. This is not all : behold where on the eaft the copious Guadalquiver rolls its majeftic flood, fertilizing the adjacent lands, while woods of olives, corn-fields, and vineyards, cover its bofom with the wealth of Spain, and lovely orange groves fringe its banks with a rich tiffue of lively green and gold; oh, it is tranfporting! here could I reft—here could I reft for ever!

Here a bell tolled for fome time—Do you not perceive, continued Alphonfo, that in the bofom of this thick wood, and beyond thofe ftately ruins rifing out of it, there muft be a place inhabited? for that is the bell either of fome nobleman's caftle or of fome neighbouring convent tolling to matins. We will fee, faid he, proceeding to mount his horfe.

Then, faid Pierrot, if it muft be fo, it muft be fo; come on, then—do as you like; it fhall never be faid that Pierrot lagged behind; or that, when hell was broke lcofe, he could not ftand fire as well as another.——No, no, if Pierrot be not as well able as e'er an Alphonfo in the

land

land (begging your honour's pardon) to endure
a flaking of fire, fword, enchantment, or demons,
let him never receive mercy.

By this time Alphonfo was mounted, and
turning his horfe towards the weft proceeded
flowly through the valley, looking ever and anon
around him, ftopping his horfe and mufing—at
one time admiring the beauty of the place, at another making fuch obfervations as he thought neceffary to a future recognition of it. He foon
perceived on his left hand a rifing ground, refembling a moat, which ftarted from the root of
the mountain, and turning his horfe afcended it:
from thence he had a more enlarged view of the
plain below, and could diftinctly obferve, at the
back of the old buildings in which he had fpent
his night, and clofe to them, a building which,
from having a belfry, he concluded to be a convent: beyond this, he thought he faw, though in-
diftinctly, marks of unufual cultivation; he therefore difmounted, and with much pains clambered
up the rocks behind, from whence he could perceive a magnificent caftle, with turrets, moats,
draw-bridge, &c, and an extenfive demefne in
high improvement behind it. He wifhed to fee
fome one to whom he could apply for information; but all near him was a blank and filent de-
fert.

fert. Come hither, Pierrot, faid he, and be com-
forted—See you yonder convent?—I do, Señor.—
Well, alight and come hither, and I will fhew you
fomething more.   Pierrot afcended to him—Do
you fee yonder caftle? That I do, your honour.—
Do you obferve the turret and draw-bridge? I
do, Señor.—Well, what think you now? Why,
I think as before ; and the more fo, on account of
that caftle—for it is there your devil's deeds are
done.—Ah, Lord! your great men with caftles
think no more of taking the lives of men, than
old women do of killing chinches, or cracking
fleas.—Lord help us! Still, I fay to your honour,
let us be gone, for there is no more mercy in
thofe caftles, than there is pity in the heart of a
witch.—Pierrot, faid Alphonfo, how fhall we find
out to whom that caftle belongs? Suppofe you
were to go thither and enquire. Why, as to that,
returned Pierrot, if your honour commands, I
will go though it were to the mouth of hell—But
I would almoft as foon lofe my life at once—nay,
I am fure I fhould never live to return to you
again.   Well, then, generous Pierrot, returned
Alphonfo, I will not command, nor even permit
you to go; but we will ride up through the wood
to thofe goatherds who fit on the hill beyond it,
and they perhaps will inform us.   Overjoyed to
be

be releafed from the vifit to the caftle, Pierrot approved of the propofal with alacrity, and they arrived at the verge of the wood, which was fo thick, that a perfon on horfeback could not make way through it; they therefore rode along it, and at laft came to a path or rather narrow road, which from its direction feemed to lead up the hill: by this path, after many windings and turnings, he got to the open fpace on the top, where he faw, not far from him, the goatherds fitting at their breakfaft. He rode up to and accofted them with his ufual courtefy, which they returned by inviting him to take a fhare of their fare. He felt himfelf not difinclined to eat, and alighting fat down cheerfully to a meal of bread and oranges, with fome poor wine: while he was making a hearty repaft upon thofe, he enquired what the name of that beautiful valley was, and whofe was the caftle? when the eldeft of the goatherds obliged him with the following recital.

CHAP.

C H A P. VIII.

The Goatherd's Story.

I AM now old, and have all my life followed the bufinefs of a goatherd, and of courfe muft have feen vaft numbers of beautiful places ; but never have I feen any place to equal in beauty this very fpot of Vallefanto ; and this, Señor, all men will tell you, was its reputation time out of mind ; and the richnefs of its paftures, the cool- nefs of its air, the plenty of its provifions, the con- tent of its inhabitants, the fanctity of its convent, and the virtues of the family who were lords of it, made it the topic of converfation in all neighbour- ing parts. The prefent lord of all the country you fee round is the Marquis de Punalada, almoft as old as myfelf : he came to the poffeffion of the eftate and caftle at an early age, and was beloved by all who knew him ; his fame was not confined to this valley, for there were few in Spain who

did

did not hear of and acknowledge his greatnefs. He married a lady his equal in rank, reputation, and fortune; but in charity, piety, and all the virtues that diftinguifh Chriftians, fuperior to all the men and women of her day. They lived long together in the greateft happinefs, and had two children, a fon and a daughter; and all the poor rejoiced in the profpect of finding one day, in the virtues of the children, a continuation of the advantages they had already derived from the charity of their forefathers. Soon after the birth of thofe children, the Marquis was called on by the king to attend him to the wars—fo he went, leaving his lady and family behind him, and from that time Vallefanto began to decay. Captivated by the king's favour, he grew proud, and forgot his good lady and children at home. However, at laft he did come—but fo different a man in his conduct from what he had been, that no one would have believed him to be the fame perfon.— The dear Marchionefs took it forely to heart, and died fuddenly—and he again was fo affected at her death that he hid from company, betook himfelf entirely to the convent, and many faid that he was going to take the cowl. However, after fome time he quitted it, and took his children to a diftant part where the king had given him a

large

large eftate; and then there were reports that
my lady's fpirit appeared at night, and made
the caftle uneafy to him: be that as it may, he
came here but feldom, and for years the children remained at his other eftate. However, at
laft he removed them here; and the caufe that
was affigned for it was fo extraordinary, that if I
had not had it from one of his own domeftics I
fhould not have believed it. In fhort, the young
lady had fallen in love defperately, and what was
worfe, hopelefsly—it was with a picture! It was
faid to be the picture of fome man dead God
knows how long. However, this did not fatisfy
the young lady, but fhe muft go to a Hadador*,
who told her, that whenever fhe fhould fee a man
who refembled that picture, the houfe of Punalada
would tumble to the ground. Some of her attendants informed the Marquis of this prediction;
in confequence of which he hurried her off here,
and fhut her up in a chamber of the caftle, where
fhe was watched with the utmoft vigilance: no
one had accefs to her but the Marquis, the Father
Prior of the convent, her brother, and fome old
domeftics; for, having in his fury ordered the
picture to be burnt, he had nothing to give the

* A fortune-teller.

fervants as a guide; whereas, had he kept the picture, he might have compared all comers with it, and so perhaps kept off danger. As misfortunes feldom come alone, the Marquis perceived a new turn in the caftle, which threatened not only forrow but fhame: in fhort, he found that my young lord, his fon, had fallen violently in love with his fifter, and was abandoned enough to make odious propofals to her. The unhappy young lady, to fhelter herfelf, told the Marquis, who directly put her into the convent; while he himfelf, racked with fome inward affliction, fhut himfelf from all intercourfe but with the Padre Prior. Meantime people gave their tongues a loofe, and talked ftrangely; the place, even the convent, was faid to be haunted; a chapel, in which mafs was fometimes celebrated, was fhut up and let to run to ruin: in fhort, Señor, nothing but misfortune, affliction, and bad luck, has for many years attended the family and the place; and the neighbouring goatherds have forfaken the valley upon account of frightful appearances that haunt it.

Do you mind that, Señor? interrupted Pierrot——Why, good man, as his worfhip and I were laft night——Alphonfo darted an angry look at him, and he was filent.

As for matter of that, continued the goatherd,

8   who

who obferved Alphonfo, the man can tell us nothing new, fo your honour need not have any fcru-
ples—there is more talk than you think of—and
in truth the Marquis is now for his tyranny, wickednefs, and morofenefs, more difliked and fuf-
pe&ed than he ever was beloved; for though we
of this place be poor, we have clear confciences,
and worfhip God and our Redeemer, and hate
wickednefs fo much, that we would not like a king
that was bad. Caltilians, thank God, are good -
Chriftians, and would not barter with the devil,
though they were to gain worlds and their wealth
by the bargain. But to conclude this ftrange
ftory, the young man, inftigated by the devil—
abandoning all fenfe of religion and virtue, and
running counter to the courfe of nature, finding
himfelf unable to prevail on his fifter to indulge
an inceftuous paffion for him, determined to enjoy
her by force or ftratagem; and to this end, with
large gifts and great promifes, bribed a fervant
who attended her to aid his defigns, and, as fhe
fince confeffed, to put a fleepy dofe in her drink,
and let him in at night.—As God, who dire&s
hings for the prote&ion of the innocent and the
unifhment of the guilty, would have it, all his
lans turned to his own ruin. Her chamber was

in

in the uppermoſt ſtory of the convent, and looked into a court-yard : by means of immenſe bribes he found his way into the yard, while his accomplice, the lady's ſervant maid, let down a ladder made of ſilk, which he had ſupplied her with, and which ſhe faſtened above to one of the iron bars of the window. He aſcended—but juſt as he got near the window the ladder gave way, he tumbled headlong down, and was caught on the ſpikes of the railing below—meantime the jade above threw out the ladder, and went to bed. In the morning his lordſhip was found dead—the Marquis was with difficulty prevented from ſlaying himſelf: an enquiry was ſet on foot, and the holy brotherhood extorted from the wretch a confeſſion. Soon after the Marquis brought from court a nephew of his, who is to inherit the eſtate, and hoped to marry him to the young lady, but ſhe abſolutely refuſed. Thus things remain at preſent—his lordſhip drags on a horrible life in his caſtle, and the young lady a wretched one in the convent.

By the time that the goatherd had finiſhed his ſtory Don Alphonſo had eaten his breakfaſt ; when riſing, and in the moſt courteous terms thanking them for their hoſpitality, and the old man in particular

ticular for his story, he mounted his horse, and
being directed in his road, took his departure,
having ordered Pierrot to give each of them a
piece of money, and the old man five.

They had not gone far, when Pierrot taking advantage of his master's indulgence began—And
now, Señor, what think you of this same Marquis de Punalada? Is it not better a thousand
times to be dead than lead such a life as he does?
And I warrant he is more careful of it too than
you or I of ours, and so it seems by his watching
—and does not that shew his wickedness? God
help him! God help him! Bad as life is, he fears
death may be worse.—Oh Lord! oh Lord! pre-
serve me from the guilt of murder!—If the devil
so far got the better of me as to make me com-
mit murder—I—I—I don't know what I should
do—I would cut a hole in the ground and bury
myself in it.—Murder!—Oh, I freeze at the very
thoughts of it. The greatest king in Christendom
could not give life to a frog or a blade of grass—
what must he be then who takes away the life
of a Christian? Yet, God help us! such is the
madness of the world, that nothing gets a man so
great a name as killing another—and the more he
kills, the greater is his honour, as you call it! Ah,

I.   Don

Don Alphonfo! quit this life of war, and lead one of bleffed peace, as a true Chriftian fhould do.

Upon my word, Pierrot, I muft allow that you apophthegmatize moft ingenioufly, but I cannot fee how that which you have faid could arife from the fubject we were talking of.

What! Does not your honour think that the Marquis has been guilty of murder? The way he lives—the haunting of the place—befides, while the old man was telling you his ftory, another of the goatherds told me as much as made my blood run cold—I may be wrong to be fure, but I would not for all the eftates and caftles in Andalufia have the confcience of the Marquis.

At laft they got into the high road, and early that evening arrived at Cordova. Here Alphonfo found himfelf divided between two duties, and debated with himfelf whether he fhould directly proceed to court to the king, or go to his father's, to throw himfelf at his feet, and, in conformity to the monition in the dream, to confult the Baron. After fome deliberation, he determined to truft rather to the tendernefs of a father than the caprice of a court, and accordingly went ftraight to Burgos, from whence he difpatched the two following letters by Pierrot:

To

To Don Isidor.

" As I approached towards home, I found my-self divided between two conflicting duties, one to my father, the other to my sovereign; and though my inclinations fought on the side of the former, prudence carried the victory in favour of the latter. The king honoured me beyond my merits, and this raised up enemies against me at court. It is to obviate their machinations that I delay the happiness of throwing myself at the feet of the best and most beloved of parents; a hap-piness, however, which I shall not deny myself many days—hoping soon to embrace you.

ALPHONSO."

To Baron de Rayo.

" A great and portentous incident, of which I hope soon to inform you, calls me to hasten to the castle of Duero; it is such as I dare not com-mit to paper, nor know I whether it should be unfolded to any one else, even to my father.—I am obliged first, however, to wait on the king; and will, as soon as I can, receive your benedic-tion in person. It is a supernatural monition I

L 2

have

have to communicate—I cannot therefore exprefs
my anxiety on that account, and am apprehenfive
of delays on the part of his majefty. If you could
prevail on Don Ifidor to accompany you to Burgos,
you might, perhaps, find the fatigue of the journey compenfated by the ftrange eventful hiftory I
have to relate, the clue of which feems referved
for you alone to unravel—I can fay no more in
this way.—Turn this in your mind, and beftow
your prayers on

ALPHONSO."

Alphonfo was received with every mark of tendernefs by the king, who informed him, that the
author of the anonymous letter was too wary to
fall into the trap projected for him—but that he
was fully convinced Don Rodrigo and his mother
were at the bottom of it. In little more than a
week after he had difpatched the letters to his father and the Baron, he had the happinefs of feeing them at Burgos. The latter was impatient
to hear the promifed ftory, and clofeted himfelf for
above an hour with Alphonfo, who gave him an
accurate account of every particular, not forget-
ting the goatherd's account of the Marquis de
Punalada.

The

The Baron, after examining and queſtioning him over and over on the ſame particulars, at length was ſilent; and, after ruminating for ſome time, deſired Don Iſidor to be called in. To him he made Alphonſo again relate the wonders of Vallefanto. Don Iſidor was aſtoniſhed. It is, ſaid the Baron vehemently, it is the blood of Gonſalvo crying from the ground!—I own it is extraordinary, ſaid Don Iſidor, who turning to Alphonſo, ſifted him with all his art; and confeſſed he ſcarcely knew what to ſay to it. Say to it! exclaimed the Baron, we will act to it: nor ſhall my ſoul find one moment's reſt, till the horrid ſecret is revealed. Don Iſidor, your whole aid is requiſite, and I demand it. Don Iſidor bowed aſſent. I requeſt, continued the Baron, that Father Thomas may forthwith be ſent for, together with one more attendant ſuch as you can depend on.— Juanico, interpoſed Alphonſo. He is the very man I wiſh, returned the Baron. Alphonſo was aſtoniſhed—he ſaw in the Baron a new man: youthful vigour re-animated every feature, enlivened every motion, and gave to his limbs a force, and to his whole air a formidable energy, that age never exhibits. Don Iſidor was delighted—he once again ſaw that Baron Rayo that uſed at once to impreſs

L 3   him

him with love and awe; and his foul again confeffed the pleafing neceffity of obedience. All
fhall be done, Baron, faid he: need I fay that my
hand, heart, and life, are devoted to the accomplifhment of your defire? Yes, yes, faid the Baron, ftriding acrofs the room; the ftains, the forrows, the difgraces, the murders, that have brought
the houfe of Rayo to the ground, though they cannot be repaired, fhall be revenged—moft horribly
revenged—and this arm fhall be the inftrument!

But, dear Baron, interrupted Don Ifidor, reprefs
this rifing choler — overcome thofe emotions,
which indulged may perhaps be the means of
fruftrating your views.

Here, faid the Baron quickly, take that hand—
does it tremble? Feel this heart—beats it a higher
or quicker pulfe than ufual? No: this that you
call emotion is the fixed temper of my foul—the
unalterable condition of my mind. By Heaven
I will mince that viper, and grind him and his
houfe, even to the laft clod of his generation,
into duft!

Don Ifidor was filent—Alphonfo felt an unufual trepidation.—The Baron feemed to tread
in air.

Pierrot was again fent back to Duero, with a
a letter

a letter to Father Thomas, who in eight days more returned, together with Juanico, to Burgos. Every neceffary preparation was made; and they, that is to fay—the Baron, Don Ifidor, Father Thomas, and Alphonfo, attended by Juanico and Pierrot, fet out for Vallefanto.

CHAP. IX.

ON the fifth day they arrived at the entrance of the valley, juft as the fun was half way dipped behind the weftern hill on which Alphonfo and his fervant had before breakfafted with the goat-herds. Don Ifidor looked about him as he advanced, wrapt in delight with the beauty of the fcene—Never, faid he, have I feen any thing to equal it! They came to a little rill of water clear as the pureft cryftal, which ran towards the river—in fome places forming the moft enchanting pools, deep, pellucid, and fheltered by hanging willows—and in others babbling over pebbles with a fweet and lulling murmur. Alphonfo had not feen it before, having entered the valley on the fouthward. This, faid he, only this was wanting to make Vallefanto more than terreftrial; let us crofs it at this fhallow ford, and fhelter us from obfervation in yonder clump of trees, while I point out to you the fituation of the place—They accordingly croffed the brook, rode up to the clump, in the heart of which they found a beautiful recefs of an almoft circular form, concealed

by

by a thickly knotted underwood from view; while an immenſe cork tree which grew in the centre of it, extending its large branches thick ſet with leaves, afforded a roof almoſt impervious to the ſight, and which promiſed a ſhelter from the ſevereſt ſtorms. Into this, after having diſmounted, they entered, and led their horſes. Alphonſo then brought the Baron, Don Iſidor, and Father Thomas forth, and pointed out to them the perpendicular angular rock—the moat—and the wood in which was buried the ſcene of their intended operations—The bell tolled—'twas for veſpers—They returned to the thicket, where Father Thomas ſaid maſs, and all joined in prayer. When the bell tolls again, ſaid Father Thomas, it will be time for us to proceed ; the Fathers will then retire to reſt, and by the time we get there all will be quiet. At length the bell tolled—the moon was quite obſcured, and but a few ſcattered ſtars lent barely light enough to direct them in their way. Leaving their attendants to take care of the horſes, they ſet out, and croſſed the plain directly towards the convent: as they approached it, they heard a foot before them treading with ſlow and heavy ſteps—they ſtood and liſtened—it ſtopped—they again proceeded—again it was heard—again they ſtopped—and

again

again it ceafed—It is the echo of our feet, faid Don
Ifidor—Why not then of all our feet? faid the Baron—It is but of one perfon. A violent ftamp of
a foot attended with the rattle of armour was
heard—We come! exclaimed the Baron in a
tone of terrific intrepidity—then turning to them
—Hafte you, let us forward—we are called. At
length they came near the wall. Beyond this, faid
Alphonfo, is the pathway—it is difficult to find
it—neverthelefs, I think I cannot fail of knowing
it. They walked flowly on: I fee a light, faid Don
Ifidor in a low voice—let us ftop—we may be difcovered.—I fee it too, faid the Baron, but fear it
not—it is friendly, let us get on. He then advanced, and broke through the bufhes, his vigour
and alacrity furprifing the reft who followed;
Father Thomas brought up the rear. Let me,
faid Alphonfo, go firft and find out the paffage. He
groped along the wall, and found out the narrow
entrance.—Here it is, faid he, follow me. They all
followed. When got into that part which he fuppofed to be the aifle—Now am I at a lofs, faid he,
to find the door into the chapel.—I have brought
a fmall lamp, faid the Baron; we will ftrike a light,
but perhaps it may difcover us. A bell tolled, and
ftraight the chapel within was illuminated—Bleffed
be God and our Redeemer! faid Father Thomas
—They

—They all faid Amen, and entered the chapel. Father Thomas advanced to the altar—knelt and prayed—They all did the fame—He faid a fhort mafs, and they arofe. Here, faid Alphonfo, here is the fpot, behold the mark of the fword. At thefe words the light was fuddenly extinguifhed, and they left in utter darknefs. The Baron then lighted his lamp, and with Father Thomas looked around—This, faid the prieft, is the weft : here muft have been the great entrance, and lo ! it is ftopped up—This then, faid he, moving on, is the north ; and what fhould bring this pile of rubbifh here, I cannot guefs, for over it there is no mark of ruins.—That we will fee, faid the Baron, let us remove it. He then drew a maffy Moorifh fabre from his fide, and fell to work loofening the rubbifh, while Alphonfo and Don Ifidor drew it away—At length the fabre met refiftance—What can this be ? faid the Baron. He worked with his hand, and felt till he found a large chink—he put in the fabre and raifed it up—It was a large ftone—Here have been much pains taken, faid he, to jam thofe ftones together. By this time he had got to the level of the floor : the Baron picked away a layer of ftones, and found another : he groped again to find a chink, but all was folid—Alphonfo knelt down and infpected it clofely : it was an immenfe

ftone

ftone of four feet in furface. We muft raife it, faid
the Baron : fee if there be any the fmalleft opening
in which to infinuate the point of the fabre.—I
cannot perceive one, faid Alphonfo, but here I fee
the upper part of a regular arch.—Where? faid the
Baron.—Here; juft where you removed the ftones.
—We muft remove that too, faid the Baron; it con-
ceals fome deed which fhuns the light. The Almighty, can, if it fo pleafe him, difclofe the ada-
mantine entrails of the earth, and fhall he not
give us ftrength to accomplifh this?—As he fpoke
thofe laft words, he fell vigoroufly to work, till
he found the under edge of the flab of ftone that
oppofed his paffage. Having made a way for their
hands, they all exerted their ftrength, lifted it up
on one end, and thence turned it over. Under-
neath was a flight of ftone ftairs going downward,
filled with rubbifh. As one only could work in fo
narrow a place, an affectionate fcuffle enfued who
that one fhould be—Alphonfo and Don Ifidor both
infifting on the Baron's yielding it to them. They
were interrupted by a noife—they liftened—a figh
which feemed to burft the bofom that it came
from filled the chapel. The Baron worked with
redoubled ardour, throwing up the rubbifh that
obftructed the ftairs—Alphonfo beheld him with
aftonifhment; the alacrity of youth and the

ftrength

ſtrength of Hercules ſeemed united in him.—Here
is a door, ſaid he. A hollow ſound within ſtopped
him: he hearkened, and diſtinctly heard the rattling
of armour, and the ſounds of haſty footſteps running to and fro—Endue me with ſtrength, ſaid he,
great Father of might ! and tore up the rubbiſh,
as the enraged lion tears up the earth with his
claws : at length he got to the door which opened
outwards, and was faſtened within. Here, ſaid
he, is a door without a key-hole or any viſible
means of opening it—If, ſaid Don Iſidor, we
could with a knife cut an entrance for our hands,
perhaps our united ſtrength might get it open.
Perhaps ſo, ſaid the Baron, but where is the
knife? Here, ſaid Father Thomas.—Don Iſidor
took the knife and deſcended : he cut for ſome
time : the impatient Baron ſnatched it from him ;
the wood flew in ſhowers of ſplinters from his
hands. At length they made room for their hands,
and the Baron, Don Iſidor, and Alphonſo tore it
open : it was faſtened by a chain hooked to a ponde-
rous ſtone within. Juſt as they opened the door a
moſt tranſporting peal of muſick ſtruck up, and
voices more than human ſung the Nunc dimittis.
They entered, drew the door after them, and
got into a paſſage arched, low, and narrow.
They went forward, the Baron with his ſword
drawn

drawn leading the way, then Alphonſo, then Don
Iſidor; and laſt, with a crucifix in his hand, Father
Thomas: at the end of the paſſage they found
a door bolted on the ſide next them. There muſt
be ſome other way that we have not yet ſeen, into
this paſſage, ſaid the Baron; for the door by which
we entered, as well as this, are bolted on the inſide. They looked attentively on either ſide, and
ſaw none. Let us open this then, ſaid the Baron.
He opened it, and they found a large extenſive
cavern filled with dead bodies in various ſtages of
diſſolution, ſome mouldered to duſt, ſome half
conſumed, and ſome again in a more offenſive ſtate
of putrefaction, lying on their backs with crucifixes
tied erect in their hands.—This, ſaid Father Thomas, is the cemetery of the convent: what ſhall we
do here? Hardly were thoſe words pronounced
when their ears were aſſailed with a violent
rattling of armour behind them: they ſtarted, and
looked round them into the paſſage they had
come through. Gracious God! exclaimed Alphonſo, there is the figure. I ſee it, ſaid the Baron, looking at it with a fixed and undiſmáyed
attention—I ſee it—Oh Iſidor, doſt thou not?—
The tears rolled in torrents down his cheeks: he
could no more, but uttered a groan that ſeemed to
have rent his ſoul from its tenement. The figure
ſtood

ſtood—All gazed in a tranſport of horror except the Baron, who ſeemed moved only by grief. It lifted. up its vizor—Oh all ye ſaints of Heaven! exclaimed Don Iſidor, is not that Gonſalvo?—The Baron put the lamp into the hands of Father Thomas, and advanced to it up the dark paſſage : preſently they heard the Baron cry out, Speak, oh ſpeak, Gonſalvo! —and inſtantly the craſh of a heavy ſuit of armour falling to the ground—Come hither, ſaid the Baron. They came up—Oh Iſidor! ſaid he, prepare yourſelf for ſuch a miraculous event as will ever ſerve to remind you of the immediate agency of the Almighty, and ſtrike ſcepticiſm and the reaſonings of pigmy men dumb; bring hither the lamp, here we muſt enter.—Why this is a wall! ſaid the Prieſt. We muſt enter it nevertheleſs, ſaid the Baron. The active mind and piercing eye of Alphonſo ended the difficulty: he found a low door, which like the firſt ſhut on the inſide, but was opened with leſs pains : the foul and condenſed air ruſhing forth blew out the lamp, and they were again in darkneſs : the young marrow of Alphonſo froze with horror, and even Don Iſidor was diſmayed.—The Baron again ſtruck a light, by which they found that they were in a ſmall vault, arched over head, and low.—Alphonſo ſtruck his foot againſt ſomething hard : he took

5

it up: 'twas a fhort fabre, the blade of which was rufty all over, but a large fpot near the end of the edge embolffed with a large raifed incruf- tation of ruft—Take that, .faid the Baron to Father Thomas, and keep it by you. The light of the lamp was too feeble to extend through the vault, fmall though it was: they therefore fearched flowly along ftep by ftep, and by the dim light it af- forded, took the beft view they could of the place. As they went along thus round the walls, Father Thomas, who ftood in the middle of the vault, ima- gined that he found the ground beneath him move: he ftruck it with his foot, and a hollow found iffued from it: he called the reft. Here is fomething, faid he, probably worth notice. They came over, and ftand- ing in turn upon it, each found it fpring beneath his feet, and heard the hollow found.—The Baron without a word began to dig away the earth: he had not removed half a foot in depth when he found a board. They all immediately affifted him, and the earth was removed from a bed of plank of feveral feet in furface: they tore it up, and beneath found a cheft in which was depofited a fkeleton, the flefh of which was quite mouldered away. It was obvioufly that of a man of extraordinary ftature. The Baron touched it, and it funk beneath his hand: he hung over it for fome time—Is there

8   not

not another, faid he, along with it ? They moved
the earth about it, but there was none. They then
turned to the cheft again : the prieft took the fkull,
which was not quite diffevered from the trunk till he
ftirred it, and attentively viewing it he perceived
that it was cloven acrofs behind. The Baron looking wiftfully at it, and fhewing it to Don Ifidor, afked him rather fternly, if he recollected any thing
about a dream — Don Ifidor bowed in humble acknowledgment — The Prieft, whofe curiofity on this
occafion feemed greateft and moft obfervant, felt
round the cheft, infpected the bones, the clothes,
and every part of it—at length, Here, faid he, is
fomewhat more than flefh and bones.—It was a feal
ring. He prefented it to the Baron, who looking
at it attentively for fome time exclaimed, O God !
then handing it over to Don Ifidor, faid, Doft thou
know this device ? What fay reafon and fcepti-
cifm now ?—Don Ifidor looked, ftarted, breathed
fhort—Do I know it ?—Yes, on my foul this is the
ring of Gonfalvo : here is his device too, a hand
and dagger, with Inftar Fulminis his motto—
Well, Don Ifidor, faid the Baron, are you now
convinced ?

Although this be fufficient to convince me, returned Don Ifidor, I think we fhould leave no
means untried to obtain every teftimony this place

M   can

can afford; let us fearch further.—I intend it, faid
the Baron.—He accordingly led them again, beginning at the door, round by the wall, viewing with
clofeft infpection the ground, and ftamping
upon it to find whether it was hollow.—At length
they came to a heap, as they thought, of earth;
the Baron ftruck it with his foot, a helmet and
coat of mail rolled about the floor—The Baron
took up one part, Don Ifidor another. It is the
armour of a giant rather than a common man,
faid the Prieft—It was my fon's, faid the Baron.
Father, lend me your knife.—He took the knife and
fcraped away the ruft: Behold, faid he, our family
device, and here read. They read aloud, Inftar
Fulminis—Yes, yes, my child! faid the Baron
vehemently; a thunderbolt thou wert to thy enemies, but treachery beguiled and deprived thee of
thy precious life; and now that arm, which carried terror to the enemies of Caftile and victory to
its banners, is fallen to a clod of the valley.—Here
the Baron's anguifh, like a ftream long ftopped in
its courfe, burft in a torrent of tears and groans,
which feemed to fhake the arches of the vault:
for fome time he was filent: at length turning to
Don Ifidor and Father Thomas, he faid, Lay them
as they were till all is ripe, and then fhall the arms
of Rayo burft like a thunderbolt upon the devoted

heads

heads of the guilty. Let us proceed. They then went further, and found a leathern portmanteau, much decayed, and full of infects: the Baron strove to open it; it broke in pieces, and a silver-hafted dagger with the aforesaid crest, a crucifix studded with rubies, and some papers fell out of it upon the ground. The Baron searched it further, and in a private flap of it found a number of papers. Those papers, said he, reverend Father, together with this cross and dagger, and the ring, we confide to you, requesting that you will seal them up—And you, Don Isidor, will witness the transaction, till justice calls them forth. They reckoned the papers, Don Isidor and Alphonso writing their names on each, and the priest took possession of them.

Although no more be necessary now, and it draws fast towards morning, said the Baron, let us leave nothing unexamined. They searched round with the most scrupulous exactness—not a spot, not a flaw in the floor or the walls that they did not examine. While they were thus engaged, the young Alphonso, who was walking to and fro, busied in contemplating the scene before him, and felicitating himself with the thoughts that he had contributed to the disclosure of such a horrid affair, struck the hilt of his sword against a part of

M 2

the

the wall, which founded very hollow, and apprifed them of it. They brought the lamp.—Affuredly, faid the Baron, my daughter was not fpared—perhaps there may be another depofitory of the dead here.—They knocked at the wall—felt it, examined it, and the more they advanced in a particular direction, the more hollow it founded.—At laft they touched a door fo neatly fitted that it feemed to be a part of the wall, but crevice or joint they could difcover none : determined, however, not to leave it unaccomplifhed, they perfifted; the prieft fcraping and probing with his knife, and the Baron with his fword, while Alphonfo looking lower difcovered a key-hole.—Let us cut it here, faid the prieft.—Hold, faid the Baron—for this perhaps our Alphonfo has already found a key. Then taking forth that which Alphonfo had found in purfuance of the monition in the dream, he tried it, and the lock flew open. Here, faid the Baron, let us look with humble adoration to the Great Difpofer of events —and henceforth let wonder ceafe—" His ways are in the great deep, and not to be fearched out :" yet man, puny creature, and arrogant as puny, will eftimate heavenly things by earthly calculations, and doubt of the extent of the power of the Almighty, only becaufe his feeble reafon cannot comprehend it.

Juft

Juſt as he was opening the door, Father Thomas ſtopped him.—Hold ! ſaid he, we go on without conſidering how many hours have elapſed ſince we entered into thoſe buildings. Morning approaches—I fear that day has already dawned—diſcovery might ruin all—therefore let us begone. You ſay well, ſaid Don Iſidor, it muſt be daybreak. Alas ! ſaid the Baron, much remains behind—and ſhall we go ?—then pauſing--Yet it muſt be.

Were I permitted to adviſe, ſaid Don Iſidor, we ſhould immediately depart, carefully laying every thing in ſuch a manner as, if ſearched, to baffle ſuſpicion. They accordingly covered up the cheſt with the earth ; Father Thomas devoutly pronouncing the Las Animas over it. They then cloſed the door of the vault, proceeded next to the ſteps up to the chapel ; where cloſing the door, and laying down the large ſtone, they put the whole, as nearly as they could, in its former ſtate, and departed.

M 3   CHAP.

CHAP. X.

THEY arrived at the bower juſt as diſtant ob-
jeſts were rendered viſible by the increaſing light
of the morning ; there they found their attendants
anxiouſly expecting their arrival, having ſuffered
much from apprehenſion as well as cold. Every
thing now, however, tended to cheer and repay
them for the hardſhips of the night. The riſing
ſun by degrees chaſed away the cold, and rendered the air moſt exquiſitely refreſhing. Ten
thouſand birds filled the air with the harmony of
nature ; from the diſtant hills was heard inceſ-
ſantly the bleating of flocks innumerable, while
the goatherds' pipe, and now and then the bark-
ing of their dogs, broke in occaſionally, and finiſhed the picture of this new Arcadia.

After having refreſhed themſelves with ſome
bread and wine which they had brought with
them, they mounted, and ſet forward towards
Burgos,

Burgos, repaſſing the river. The Baron muſed for ſome time; at laſt breaking ſilence, and turning to the others behind him, Behold, ſaid he, how magnificently the hand of the Creator has furniſhed the abodes of all his creatures! Not all the embelliſhments of art, ſtrained to the laſt nerve of human ſkill, not all the proud domes, raiſed ſtory over ſtory by the aſpiring hand of architecture, not gilded cielings, burniſhed arches, columns of poliſhed marble, gold or ſilver moulded by the hand of taſte and inſcribed with the proud emblems of nobility, can be put in compariſon with this one ſmall ſpeck in the works of Omnipotence: nay, let but the hand of art touch it, and its beauties vaniſh!—Hark! every throat of the pretty feathered tribe ſwelled inſtinctively with notes of grateful adoration! The flocks bleat forth their praiſe—the noble ox, his appetite and mere corporeal functions all ſuſpended in mute devotion, contemplates the beauties that ſurround him, heaves his huge ſides with rapture, and in enjoyment pays his tribute to the hand that feeds him! Man, only man, ſwollen with the pride of reaſon (that dubious inſtrument, by Heaven given, his bleſſing or his curſe), becomes the bubble of creation—ſinfully ſpurns from him gifts like thoſe, and

M 4

to his own gaudy perishable works resorts for satisfaction—worse ! strains his prolific mind for
means to desolate the face of fair creation—for
spurious pleasures, which baffle in pursuit or poison in enjoyment, wages inexorable war against
the will of Heaven, spreads his own brother's
couch with serpents' teeth—ravages — ruins—murders !———

Just as he had pronounced those last words,
they came to a beautiful recess, resembling a stage
formed by the hand of nature, at the foot of the
mountain; round it the hills rose in a gentle
slope like the seats of an amphitheatre, and in the
centre of it stood a large stone cross ; the whole
was surrounded by a prattling rivulet, which fell
from the hills behind in a beautiful cataract; at
the bottom, separating into two branches, glided
round this natural stage, and meeting again below it in one stream fell into the river Guadalquiver at the distance of about a league: the
whole was surrounded by stately cork trees, which
lent a cool shade from the intense heat of the meridian sun. In this romantic spot was collected
a crowd of men and women, dressed in all the fan-
tastic finery of the country, and bedecked with
boughs and flowers: one man, who seemed the

2   chief,

chief, carried a garland in his hand, and, mated
with a beautiful female, led them all in mazes
through a dance. Don Ifidor ftopped and looked
on—Nothing, faid he, delights me fo much as an
affemblage of happy faces. The dance ftopped,
and the people faluted our travellers with ruftic
civility. Pr'ythee, faid Don Ifidor, what is the
occafion of this mirth and dancing to-day? Is it
your tutelar faint's day?. .

Why, you muft know, Señor, that the village
you fee yonder is called Villaverde: it has been
in the poffeffion of the prefent family ever fince the
expulfion of the Moors from this part of Spain:
and if the bleffed Virgin condefcends to hear the
prayers of its inhabitants, it will continue fo for
ever—for never were people fo bleffed as they are
in a lord, and never was a family-fo bleffed in return as they—if good works, the prayers of mankind, the fmiles of heaven, and being true Chriftians and real hidalgos can make them fo. Search
out the beft man in Spain, and we will fet the
worft of this family againft him, and not be afraid
of the comparifon; and of all of them that ever
poffeffed the eftate, the prefent Marquis feems the
beft; for, to the natural greatnefs of his blood,
and the hereditary goodnefs of his heart, he
unites the gifts of his good uncle Jerome, prior

of

of our convent, under whofe care he was bred :
you need not doubt then his being a good Chriftian,
which you know is faying every thing. As foon
as he came of age, inftead of lavifhing the great
wealth he got into poffeffion of, in feafts and
revels and riot, in horfes, dice, cards, or women, he laid it all out in charity, referving to himfelf no more for his expences than the pooreft
hidalgo in the country : he provides for the old
and infirm, gives inftruments of hufbandry to
young farmers, and tools to young tradefmen :
he gives portions to young maids to procure them
good hufbands, and on their marriage fupplies
them with a capital to fet them going : not a
perfon in the country but can bear teftimony to
his charity : even the little children flock about
him as he walks the ftreets, fkipping for joy like
young lambkins after their dams, and get their
quarto or ochavo to regale : in fhort, Sir, nothing,
not even the brute creation fails to find tender protection and fhelter from him * :—he is fplendid in
gifts to the church to pray for the dead, but he
is chiefly applauded for his munificence to poor
hidalgos whofe families have fallen by mifchance

* This is exactly the character of the prefent Marquis
of Villaverde, at leaft of him who lived in 1781.

or error into poverty—All men adore him—and
the Almighty has marked him for his own. Well,
Sir, this day he is to be married—the whole neigh-
bourhood is in one tumult of joy—grandees come
from all parts of the country; even the Marquis
de Punalada, who has lived like a hermit fince
the death of his wife, comes forth to add to the
meeting: all ftrangers pafling by are invited;
and the Marquis and his uncle will both be much
pleafed, and think it a great favour, if you, cavaliers, would delay your journey, and go to the
caftle of Villaverde.

That is impoffible, faid Don Ifidor; bufinefs of
confequence obliges us to return with hafte; we
wifh the worthy Marquis all the felicity fuch virtues merit, and will offer up our prayers to the
Virgin to blefs his nuptials. However, I thank
you for the pains you have taken to inform me,
and requeft that you will accept this—giving him
a piece of money—and make merry with it on
another occafion. Then turning their horfes they
proceeded on their journey.

They had not gone far when they obferved an
inn which ftood juft at the point of two roads:
here they refolved to refrefh themfelves after the
fatigues and fafting of the night: they accordingly ftopped, and having retired into a private room

I   held

held a conference on the fubject of the night's adventures. From what we have feen, faid the Baron, no doubt remains of the truth of my fufpicions: that Gonfalvo has been murdered moft foully, is certain—that the fkeleton in the cheft is his, the ring is fufficient proof; not to mention (looking at Don Ifidor) the cloven fkull, the portmanteau, and the armour; and that the Marquis de Punalada has been the murderer, is little lefs a matter of certainty. They all affented to thofe propofitions: the queftions then to be refolved are—Firft, how it has happened that the Priory fhould be made the fcene of flaughter—a place as one would think too holy for fuch deeds of darknefs; next, what provocation or inducement brought on the murder; and laftly, what has been the fate of my daughter? All thefe things remaining ftill in obfcurity, makes me wifh to return to-night to the vault—perhaps we may difcover further.

In my opinion, faid Don Ifidor, the development of all you mention hangs entirely on the difcoveries we have already made. Inftead therefore of making an unavailing journey to the vault, we fhould, in purfuance of our firft plan, proceed to court, and give the king a full and circumftantial relation of the facts from the beginning.

And

And defire him, faid the Baron, to open the lifts, and permit me to call the villain to a public vindication of himfelf in fingle combat. I think that you miftake me yet, interrupted Don Ifidor —Single combat indeed!—No, far be it from me to think of ftaining the noble warrior's fword with the blood of a murderer!—No, let juftice——

Hear me, Don Ifidor, interrupted the Baron— hear my fixed refolves—He muft fall by this arm —I cannot become an affaffin or an executioner— therefore I muft fight him—fear not thou the event—in fuch a caufe, a pigmy's arm would wreft victory from a giant: befides—but thou thinkeft that I am old—too old to—It may be fo— but know, Ifidor, that even at this age, that man bears not arms in Spain from whofe creft Rayo would not now, even now, old though he be, hope to pluck the laurel.

My dear Baron, returned Don Ifidor, I muft fay you ftill miftake me. Of the event of a com- bat I have no doubt; and if, as you feem to fur- mife, I had any that arofe from an apprehenfion of your age, I fhould, and I hope you believe it, myfelf ftep forward as the champion of our caufe. The procefs you propofe would fmother future difcovery, and many things of greateft moment, perhaps even your daughter's life (for who knows
but

but fhe yet may live ?) might all be loft in this one rafh act.—Confider, Baron, it is not a mere point of honour you have to difcharge—it is not a doubtful claim on juftice you have to enforce— you are not fo deftitute of proof as to refort to the fword—no, your proofs are already in your reach, and juftice to your whole family demands that your oppreffor fhould be brought, not to the honourable iffue of the fword, but to the ignominious fentence of the law. As to your age, Baron, it has nothing to do with it; for, in a cafe where the demands of honour called forth the fword, I know not the hand more fit to draw it than yours—If it failed, and mine fhould fink after it, remember that I have a fon.——Ay, Ifidor, you have a fon—fuch a fon as I once had —one to whofe arm the fate of empires might be trufted; but believe me, you have fhaken my intentions for the prefent. My daughter may live, faid you not fo? Look you, Ifidor, accuftomed as thou haft been to read my heart, which ever has been written in my actions, thou canft not but have obferved how much more precious than life, nay than ten thoufand lives, has honour ever been in my opinion; yet would I, to make good that one tranfporting hope—to fave my daughter—to hug her once more in thefe arms—give life, fame,

fortune,

fortune, every thing to the winds; forego all honours, all worldly hopes, and take the fate of the
moſt forlorn wretch that draws exiſtence from the
pity of mankind——But it may not be—ſhe muſt
be gone—ſhe was' not ſpared!

However, ſaid Don Iſidor, though unlikely, it
is not impoſſible: is it not better to proceed by
ſuch temperate means as may inſure our work at
leaſt from further miſchief? I ſay then, we muſt
deſire the interference of the king, and even this
muſt be done with caution, for Don Rodrigo
is nephew and preſumptive heir to the Marquis;
and his mother, who is above all women crafty,
may by circumſpection diſcover, and by addreſs
defeat us. My advice therefore is, that we re-
pair to Burgos, and that Alphonſo gain a private
audience of the king, and prevail upon him to
grant you a hearing, in which caſe there does not
remain a doubt of juſtice being done.

Father Thomas and Alphonſo added the weight
of their opinion to this advice, and the Baron
agreed. Meantime, ſaid Don Iſidor, let us take
ſome refreſhment; remain here this night to'reſt,
and early to-morrow ſet forward on our journey.

Juſt at that moment, they obſerved from their
windows a cloud of duſt ariſing at a diſtance,

and

and moving towards them; they foon heard the trampling of horfes, and prefently faw a carriage drawn by fix mules, and furrounded by armed men; it drove by the inn, and turned towards the town of Villaverde. They called their hoft, and afked him whofe it was: he anfwered, that it was the Marquis de Punalada, who for a wonder, faid he, appears abroad, going I fuppofe to the wedding: ay, ay, he has armed men enough to keep off the ghofts.—Oh Lord fave us, and keep us a clear confcience!

This Marquis then, faid Don Ifidor, is much afraid of ghofts, is he? Afraid, Señor! Why, he is the talk of the whole country, replied the hoft; we have fometimes fuch work with him—it was but a few nights ago he called up all the fervants in the middle of the night—faid that fome one was going to kill him—made them arm themfelves, and fearch all round the caftle—and at laft could not be perfuaded but that fome perfon had come to him as he lay in bed, and fhook a bloody poniard over him, threatening him with fpeedy death: he keeps almoft continually locked up in private places, and never walks even in the great gardens, though walled with battlements, without two chofen domeftics. Sometimes he difappears for days together, and is not feen by any one,

one, and the people of the caſtle think that he is
then with Father Gregorio the prior—though how
he gets there they cannot tell, as the walls of the
caſtle are between them. Be this as it will, one
of the lay-brothers ſaw him once in the prior's
cell, at a time that he had not paſſed the gate.
Some ſay that he deals with the devil—ſome ſay
one thing, ſome ſay another—ſome talk of my
lady's death—but as for me, Señors, remember, I
ſay nothing: beſides, now I think on it, you are
ſtrangers to me, and might do me a miſchief; but
thank God I can keep a ſecret. We, returned
Don Iſidor, we are above doing you a miſchief,
and hope you will not think ſo ill of us ; ſo, if you
have a ſecret——Lord! no, your honour, no
ſecret—what every one knows is no ſecret——
Why he ſcreeches, and talks to himſelf, and ſays
the wickedeſt things when he thinks that no one
is in hearing—ſuch as that God cannot pardon
him, and the like—Deſpair you know is one of
the ſeven deadly ſins—as for my part, I would not
take the wealth of Spain to be in his ſkin this
night ; for though I do keep an inn, I am an honeſt man, and never committed murder. Murder! exclaimed Don Iſidor—why, did the Marquis?. No, no, your honour—oh no—not as one
would ſay—God forbid I ſhould ſay ſo—but then

N   when

when a man is afraid of his own fhadow, and
fhrieks—I underftand you, faid Don Ifidor, touching his lips with his fingers, by way of denoting
filence—You are a wife fellow, and I commend
you.

But, Señores, continued the hoft quite flattered,
only think of his immuring his daughter, a fweet
young lady, in a cell of a convent, only out of
fear of a prophecy of a curfed witch—But that coft
his fon his life, who was—but, God forgive him!
he is dead. Then there is a poor youth he has
bred up for charity : fome fay he is his own baf-
tard—but I cannot believe it, he is too good for
that : be that as it may, he treats him cruelly.
Sometimes when he meets him he fcreeches, and
orders him to be turned out, then again fends and
has him brought back, for the lad would be glad
to go : and would you believe it? one day about
four days ago he was miffed ; meffengers were
fent to fearch for him ; they found him in a broken
building behind the convent, where he was looking for birds' nefts : and only think, the Marquis
was going to poniard him, and at laft laid him
in irons, calling him villain, cut-throat, traitor !—
Lord help us ! the boy would not cut the throat
of a chicken, though he wanted his dinner by it :
not but the fellow is brave enough, and now that
he's

he's grown is as strong as a mule. It is not six months ago since a great gang of robbers descended from the Sierra Morena, and plundered the whole country, carrying away every thing, cattle, corn and all. The Marquis was then abroad, that is to say, buried in his castle: what does the young Fernando, but claps on a suit of armour, and at the head of a few peasants sallied forth, attacked the banditti, took their chief, and kept him hostage at a small village till all they had remaining of the stolen property was restored ! The Marquis being informed of it, sent to have the fellow detained just as all was returned: but Fernando said that he had already passed his word, and would send his spear through any one that should presume to detain him ; adding, that it was better to have the things restored to their poor owners, than to hang such a worthless wretch ; and then dismissed him with an earnest exhortation to reformation and repentance. All people were astonished at the grandeur of his sentiments, particularly as he was a foundling, and, as the saying is, begot in sin :—but as soon as he went home the Marquis became outrageous, threatened him with death, laid him in irons, and kept him on bread and water for a month. When let at liberty, he walked about sad and silent, and spoke to no

N 2   one.

one. One day fauntering down a long lobby in the caftle, the Marquis fuddenly opened a room door juft facing him, fcreeched, and almoft fell into fits at the fight of him. The caftle was alarmed: his lordfhip declared that he was watching there to affaffinate him: the youth called Heaven to witnefs his innocence, and begged that he might be permitted to withdraw from the caftle, and eafe his lordfhip's mind, who feemed to abhor the fight of him: affuring him that, though grateful for paft favours, he was weary of fuch continual ill ufage; upon which the Marquis fwore he fhould never go outfide the walls of the caftle, and gave orders for his being ftrictly watched. Ever fince he remains there as it were a prifoner—he is feen fometimes walking on the battlements attended by two men as guards— no one can tell the caufe of this, but every one knows it can be nothing good.

You intereft me much in the fate of this youth, faid Don Ifidor; and your account aftonifhes me beyond meafure. There is fomething in the Marquis's conduct to him fo far furpaffing the bounds of common malignity, that, coupled with his terrors and fcreechings, denotes fome guilty myftery.

Why, Señor, faid the innkeeper, he feems almoft as much afraid of every body—nay, for

matter

matter of that, of himself; for he cannot abide to be alone at night. Indeed most of the domestics are terrified at night, and declare that the whole castle and its gardens, nay, the whole priory and valley, are haunted. Well, thank God, the Marquis of Villa-verde is my lord! I would, not be under the other for—for—for—no no, not for—Here he was called, and obliged to leave his company, and his story unfinished.

A strange account this! said Don Isidor.

A very natural one, said the Baron. Though guilt bury itself in the unfathomable abysses of the deep, it cannot fly from that awful tribunal erected for its punishment in the heart of the offender—I mean the conscience, all powerful conscience, which can smooth the rude front of adversity, and turn the hard couch of poverty into a bed of down, or goad the guilty wretch of state with stings and tortures; convert to gall the sweets which nature pours into his cup; 'midst hosts of slaves that bend at his nod, appall him with menaces of vengeance, paint to his panic-stricken soul a dagger pointed to his throat by every hand, and give him even here a foretaste of perdition. Gracious Heaven! what infatuation! that man, so oft, so awfully admonished, will not reflect—but for the shadow of some transitory pleasure, the substance

of

of which flies but the farther from his grafp, at once render this life too hideous to be borne, and preclude his wretched foul from fhelter in another!

I cannot account for it, faid Don Ifidor, but I feel a propenfity which I cannot overcome, to go towards the caftle and take a view of it. The unmerited fate of that youth, who from our hoft's account feems to have fomething noble in his foul, fills me with, I cannot fay how, an ardent wifh to fee him. Were I fuperftitious, I fhould deem thofe defires predictive—Perhaps! nay it eannot be—What? faid the Baron haftily:

In truth, replied Don Ifidor, my thoughts were fo abfurd that I almoft blufh to own them. If this fhould be your orphan grandfon!—A flufh of red crimfoned the cheek of the Baron—What! if it fhould—but oh it cannot be—why keep him there? And yet his jealous apprehenfions, his fhrieks of horror—but it cannot be—No, Ifidor! no, when he had gone fo deep in guilt as to murder the father and mother, he would not ftop at the child: much lefs would he keep him as a continual memento of his guilt—No, no, it cannot be, it cannot be! The will of Heaven be done! To it I will (I truft, with fortitude) fubmit; and, when the debt of vengeance to my murdered children is paid, bury if I can all remembrance of them

in

in their grave, and look upon Alphonſo as my child, the kindly gift of the Supreme to ſmooth the down-hill path of my declining years.

Yet, ſaid Don Iſidor, ſuppoſe we go ? It can do no injury, and will at leaſt give us a more perfect idea of the ſituation of the caſtle, to ſerve us on a future occaſion.

I agree, replied the Baron : let us go.

As ſoon as they had dined, they departed for the caſtle : as they approached it they ſaw, or thought they ſaw, the country become more gloomy; and their imagination, influenced by their opinion of the Marquis, viewed it as a place cut off from the goods of Providence, where graſs grew not, and where the affrighted earth drew back into her womb her natural produce, as fearful to truſt it to the hands of ſuch a monſter. They rode along the walls, and perceived that they were ſtrongly intrenched behind a deep ditch, over which as they advanced they found a draw-bridge drawn up : paſſing further on, they obſerved that the wall turned to the ſouthward, and continuing their route along it ſaw that it joined that of the priory. They turned back again, and as they approached the draw-bridge obſerved three men walking on the wall : on their nearer approach, Don Iſidor courteouſly ſaluting them inquired to

N 4 whom

whom that noble caſtle belonged. One of them
returned the ſalute, and informed him that it belonged to the Marquis de Punalada; that the
Marquis was from home : and ſaid, that he was
ſorry the arrangements of the caſtle forbad him
from inviting them during the Marquis's abſence.
Our travellers had not the ſmalleſt doubt, from
the youthful voice and manner of the ſpeaker, but
that he was the young perſon of whom ſuch honourable mention had been made by the inn-keeper:
Don Iſidor therefore accoſted him. Young gentleman, ſaid he, though I ſhould be ſorry to break in
upon the arrangements or treſpaſs on the privi-
leges of the caſtle, I cannot help entreating that
you would have the goodneſs to direct us in the
road to Cordova, from which, I know not how,
we have inſenſibly diverged; and as the roads
about here are rather intricately croſſed and mixed
with each other, you would conſiderably augment
the favour by deſcending, and inſtructing us particularly how we may avoid going again aſtray.
We are travellers, and, like all travellers who hope
to profit by their toil, wiſh to get the beſt account
poſſible of the country which we paſs through ;
and here have been unable to find any but uncouth
and ignorant peaſants, incapable of inſtructing us.
You honour me much, returned the youth, by your
invitation,

invitation, but there are reafons why I cannot avail myfelf of it. Juft as he faid this, one of the men who was along with him fpoke to him in a whifper—the three confulted together, and then making a fign to Don Ifidor to wait, they defcended, and letting down the draw-bridge paffed over. The young man ftepped forward and joined the Baron and Don Ifidor. As he approached, the whole company riveted their eyes upon him, and were much pleafed and indeed furprifed at the dignity of his mien, the firmnéfs of his deportment, the vigour of his limbs, and the noble manly expreffion of his countenance, in which ftrong character was deeply marked. The Baron felt a lively emotion of tendernefs towards him—Don Ifidor not lefs—while Father Thomas had all thofe fenfations that a good heart meliorated by Chriftianity may be fuppofed to feel for virtue groaning under oppreffion. They difmounted from their horfes, and leaving them to the care of the fervants walked afide with him. He began to fpeak—but an unaccountable fenfation broke his utterance, and alternately overfpread his face with a fhifting red and white : however, he informed them that this was the caftle of Punalada, as he had faid before, and that it was furrounded with walls a confiderable length backwards, even to

the

the ground of the convent of Vallefanto: that the
Marquis was a man of immenfe eftates and great
wealth, highly favoured by the court, but yet fo
fond of retirement that he chofe rather to live here
for many years paft, than go into the world and
affume that figure in it which his rank and fortune
entitled him to. You are his fon then, I prefume?
faid Don Ifidor. No, Sir; I am indeed the creature of his adoption, preferved by his charity, and
now fupported by his bounty; but whofe fon I am,
alas! I know not, nor perhaps fhall ever know:
at prefent the Marquis by his adoption is entitled to
all thofe duties which I fhould pay to my natural
parents, perhaps to more. Then you are happy?
faid the Baron. The youth hefitated—at length,
If, faid he, I anfwer in the negative, let me be
acquitted of any intentional ingratitude to my pro-
tector. I have never gone fo far before, and I
confefs I am aftonifhed to think by what irrefiftible
power your notice of me exacts a confeffion which
I have never made to any one. The Marquis
has been kind to me—I owe him every thing, yet
am not happy. Why, my child? faid the Baron
earneftly. I wifh, replied the youth, to ferve my
king, and be a foldier; but I am not permitted:
the Marquis (for what reafon I cannot tell) is
averfe to it—it is his will I fhould not go, and I

muft

muſt ſubmit.—Apprehending, as I ſuppoſe, that I
have formed a deſign to depart for that purpoſe,
without his permiſſion, he has ordered me to keep
within the walls of the caſtle, and aſſigned me a
guard: but he need not; I think obedience to his
will a duty, and no earthly conſideration ſhall
make me guilty of a breach of it. Nothing could
equal their aſtoniſhment at the noble ſentiments
and ingenuous ſpirit of ſo young a man. The
Baron gazed upon him as if his eyes had loſt their
wonted motion—Don Iſidor took him by the
hand, preſſed it, and ſaid—Unhappy parents, who-
ever they are, to have loſt ſuch a ſon; and happy
he who has acquired ſuch a one, even by adoption!

The Marquis, interrupted the Baron, muſt be
ſenſible of the treaſure he poſſeſſes—He is fond of
you, my child, is he not? Alas, venerable Sir! replied the youth, he on the contrary ſeems to abhor me, and (why, I know not) to conſider me
as a perſon unworthy of truſt or confidence—
as a villain—as a traitor. Here his colour ſhifted
to a deadly pale, and a tear guſhed in ſpite of him
from his eyes, while every muſcle of his face
ſeemed agitated. In ſhort, Sirs, continued he, to
be plain, the Marquis has of late ſo treated me,
that every tie of affection is broken, and the only

ligament

ligament which now remains to bind me to him is gratitude; a bond which no true Chriſtian can break. I truſt that God will grant me the grace never to violate it. Thus have I, Señors, ſeduced by an unaccountable feeling which draws me to you with reſiſtleſs force, deviated from my accuſtomed maxims of ſilence. To have at once repoſed in you the ſecret of my heart appears now ſtrange to myſelf—yet does it not give me one painful ſenſation; on the contrary, I feel more tranquil at heart than I have for a long, long time been.

Fear not, excellent young man! ſaid Don Iſidor: you ſpeak to men of honour; nay more, you ſpeak to thoſe who feel their hearts entwined with yours in the reciprocal folds of affection, equally ſtrong as yours—equally unaccountable to themſelves.

Let us, ſaid the Baron, call you child: if affection entitles to that appellation, we claim a ſtronger right than the Marquis.

And at all events, ſaid Don Iſidor, remember that if the caprice of the Marquis, his death, or any other circumſtance, ſhould leave you at liberty to make a choice, Don Iſidor de Haro will be ready to take upon him the office of the father and the friend; and will diſcharge both to you as though you were the iſſue of his own loins.

Don

Don Ifidor, you would engrofs all to yourfelf, faid the Baron; you muſt allow the claim of the childlefs to be paramount to yours, and fuch is mine. My child, for I will call you fo, faid he, I am old, and can inftruct you; therefore hear me attentively: hope not that time, reafon, or moral or religious fentiment can work any change in the Marquis's heart in thy favour. To ufe the helplefs orphan of his protection with inhumanity, and put bonds upon his mind and perfon, ſhews him to poffefs a foul either naturally depraved, or labouring under fome malignant fufpicion or hidden animofity which broods in his heart, but dares not appear: and truſt me, youth, man in intercourfe with man feldom refts at the firſt ftage of good or evil; but where he confers an unmerited benefit, or offers an unprovoked injury, carries the folly of the one act, or the wickednefs of the other, to extremes—Never did I know a man that did not delight in foftering the worſt brier that he had planted; never do I remember a man who could forgive the innocent he had injured. Let this be your caution, this the guide of your confcience: that gratitude, which has outlived affection, is a mere religious duty, and, like that of forgivenefs of our enemies, extends not to felf-injury, involves no pofitive efteem, enjoins no pofitive at-

5

tachment,

tachment, but merely bids that we pray for and
wiſh rather good than evil to its object. In this am
I right, Father? ſaid he, turning to the prieſt. Perfectly, returned Father Thomas. One word more,
ſaid the Baron, taking him by the hand : Fly this
caſtle, as you value life, or wiſh for the protection
of Heaven—guilt ſaps its walls, vengeance holds
its ſword over it, and the thunder of Heaven ere
many days be paſt will ſhake it to its foundation.
—Fly, therefore—quickly fly—and when once thy
reſolution ſhall be taken, let this (giving him a
ſcrip of paper) be thy guide.

The youth looked with aſtoniſhment at the
Baron as he ſpoke—he was overawed by the
dignity of his looks, while the words he ſpoke
ſunk to the inmoſt receſſes of his ſoul. Don
Iſidor, continued the Baron, we muſt have this
youth between us; for as of Alphonſo, ſo of
him, neither of us will give up his ſhare. And
you, ſaid he, my children, taking both their hands
and putting them into each other, remember, that
after this day, if ever you ſhould happen to meet,
you meet as brothers. With joy, ſaid Alphonſo,
I accept from your hands that which was before
denied to me—a brother. And I, ſaid Fernando,
with gratitude for the acquiſition, earneſtly hope
that I may be worthy of it.

At

At this inftant, one of the fervants called out, Don Fernando, it is time to return; you know what wou'd be the confequence if we were detected here. I fhall return directly, faid Fernando. Then turning to the Baron and Don Ifidor, Your advice, Señors, is engraven on my heart; and if I fhould fail in perfuading the Marquis to let me forth, depend upon it I fhall take a proper opportunity to claim your protection: meantime may Heaven protect you, and grant you all the happinefs you deferve! Reverend Father, faid he, turning then to the prieft, your blefling.—God blefs you, my fon! faid the prieft. And now, my brother, fince you allow me to call you fo, faid he to Alphonfo, let us embrace and part. He then turned from them, called his attendants, and tripping over the draw-bridge hauled it up, waved his hand as a laft adieu, and difappeared.

Our travellers had not gone far from the caftle, the Baron ever and anon tolling up his eyes to heaven and groaning, and Don Ifidor in mute contemplation—when Pierrot, touching Alphonfo on the arm, and making him one of his fignificant becks to drop behind, fays, in a low tone of voice, his eyes ftaring, his mouth round as a circle, and his brows lifted up in aftonifhment, Anfwer me, Señor, only two queftions which I fhall put to you—

you—Is this country all enchanted, or is it not? that is one? And who, tell me, who do you think that young cavalier is like? that is another. Let me fee whether we be all bewitched, or whether it is me alone that the devil plays his pranks with. And is this, faid Alphonfo, the caufe of your important beckon to me to fall behind with you? To what end tend thofe two ridiculous queftions?

I'll tell you what, Señor, if you were to hang or burn me, I cannot but think that I am bewitched—for, when that youth appeared, and I firft faw him, I wiped my eyes again and again—and I doubted whether I was awake—But to the very laft I was bewitched; for, if I was not, how could he appear to me to be my mafter Don Ifidor?

Why, Pierrot, faid Alphonfo, looking earneftly in his face, are you out of your fenfes? What ftrange notion is now running in your precious noddle?

May I never live, replied Pierrot, if that young cavalier did not feem to me to be the very fame man that carried away my lady, your mother, from her father's, near Talavera—that married her—that afterwards begat you—and that is now there riding before us! Nay, your honour need not ftare, for to be fure it is all bewitchment and forcery;

for

for there is nothing about us here but conjurers, magicians, spirits, and witches, and I wish we were well out of it: nay, for matter of that, I did not like your embracing the young fellow, who, for ought we know, may be something bad, and has taken upon him that handsome shape only to hurt and deceive us : indeed, indeed, we ought to turn back, and not go the road he directed us.

Alphonso, seriously alarmed, spurred his horse and rode up to the others, and in terms of affection and tenderness deplored the insanity of Pierrot, told them the whole of what had passed, and besought them to examine him. Did I not tell you, said the Baron to Don Isidor, never did I see so strong a resemblance—that of this youth to Gonsalvo is not greater than that of Fernando to you. It is a strange mysterious business— would that we could get to the bottom of it !

O   CHAP,

CHAP. XI

As soon as they arrived at the city of Burgos, the Baron, Don Ifidor, Father Thomas, and their attendants, remained at an inn, while Alphonfo went to court. He firft made it his bufinefs to fee his patron, Don Juan de Padilla, and befought him to obtain for him a private audience of the king, to whom, he faid, he fhould, in his prefence, unfold a bufinefs no lefs furprifing than horrible. The king, not lefs inclined to oblige his minifter than to ferve his favourite, inftantly granted him the audience, in prefence of Don Juan. Alphonfo began by entreating his majefty to believe, that nothing lefs than a bufinefs of the moft ferious moment could induce him to call upon his majefty's attention in fo very ferious and urgent a manner.—He plighted himfelf to prove, to the conviction of the world, one of the moft execrable confpiracies that ever was conceived by man in his moft abandoned wickednefs—a confpiracy

formed

formed againſt the honour, the fortunes, and
the lives of a houſe diſtinguiſhed in the ſer-
vice of the crown of Caſtile—carried into effect—
concealed for many years, and at length diſcovered
by means more than ordinary—by the interven-
tion of the avenging hand of Heaven. He ſaid,
that the affair was ſo intricate, ſo dependent on a
variety of proofs, and ſo very difficult of expla-
nation, that it would be neceſſary, as well for his
majeſty's caſe as for the more perfect elucidation
of it, to have the principal perſonages of it before his majeſty : and he earneſtly entreated to
have the liberty of bringing them on the morrow
in attendance before him : one of them was Don
Iſidor, his father ; another, the Reverend Father
Thomas Auguſtino ; the third, Baron de Rayo.—
How ! ſaid Don Juan, Baron de Rayo ! Has he
not been dead, his eſtates confiſcated; and his titles
extinct ? That the Baron's eſtates were confiſcated, and his blood attainted by Peter, ſaid Alphonſo, is too true; but it is equally true that
he lives; and that the attainder was taken off by
our late king Henry. The conſpiracy and conſequent frauds and murder that led to that——
How—murder ! exclaimed the king. Even ſo, my
liege—moſt foul murder, perhaps worſe, returned
Alphonſo : I ſay, and I undertake at the hazard

of

of my life, and, what I value more, your majefty's favour, to prove that the houfe of Rayo has funk beneath the hands of a villain and a murderer!

This is ftrong language! faid the king.

It is my liege, faid Don Juan, and fuch as I prefume Alphonfo, ere he uttered it, was prepared to make good.

Then what is the fcope of your prefent demand? faid the king.

That the perfons I have named be permitted, on the morrow, to come before your majefty, in prefence of Don Juan, and fuch other perfons as your majefty may think fit, there to lay before you the whole of this tranfaction.

I grant it, faid the king.

May your faithful fervant, faid Alphonfo, pre-fume to fuggeft the neceffity of fecrefy for the prefent; Don Rodrigo is nearly concerned in the event, though not in the guilt.

Enough, faid the king—To-morrow morning at ten o'clock, I will, for greater caution, be at Don Juan's houfe; there we will hear of this ex-traordinary affair.

On the morning, Alphonfo, attended by Don Ifidor, the Baron, and Father Thomas, repaired to Don Juan's, who received them all with every mark of efteem, and particularly treated the Baron with

with diftinguifhed refpe&: they difcourfed upon the bufinefs in hand, and Don Juan affured them of the king's refolution to render juftice to the Baron.

At the appointed time the king came, and with him the corregidor of Burgos. The king defired Alphonfo to proceed. Alphonfo entreated that the Baron de Rayo might be permitted to explain the nature of the cafe. The Baron began from the very commencement, and after deprecating the impu-tation of egotifm, if he fpoke of himfelf, which the nature of the cafe demanded, gave a detail of the fervices of himfelf and his family to the ftate; relating various victories which had been ac-knowledged by the reigning kings to have been gained over the enemies of the faith and ftate, by his valour and wifdom; for a proof of all which he referred to exifting records, and living evidence. He then defcribed the heroifm and achievements of his fon; and drew a picture of the fufferings of him and his daughter, which affected the king extremely: he then adverted to his own miferies —his imprifonment—wanderings—wants—and fi-nally his reception by Don Ifidor.

Here Alphonfo took up the affair, with an ac-count of the incidents at Vallefanto.

Don Ifidor then began with the ftory of the

O 3   fearch—

fearch—and laftly, Father Thomas produced the ring, fabre, crucifix, and dagger, and the papers' found in the portmanteau, fealed up; all of which they jointly and feverally fwore to.

Don Juan was aftonifhed.—He faid, that the leading circumftances of the tale tallied exactly with facts in his recollection. He was intimate with Gonfalvo—knew his device—believed it was his ring—would certainly know his armour, as they had often fought together—and he particularly recollected, that the Marquis de Punalada fuddenly retired from court foon after the difappearance of Gonfalvo.

From the letters, which were almoft fallen to pieces, were collected the following fentences.

LETTER I.

" You have not an hour to lofe, Gonfalvo— Padre Pablo will tell you all——Hafte you away— a moment's delay may put your wife beyond your power—in the embraces of the K——."

LETTER II.

[Opened the fecond, but probably the firft in point of date.]

" There is a convent, with the prior of which I have fome power—two of my domeftics will
attend

attend you there—no other place affords you a
fanctuary againft the difappointed luft of P——
(meaning Peter)."

LETTER III.

" Leave it to me to develope the affair to the
Baron.—All your property, papers, &c. I will
fecure for you. Depend on the continuation of
my good offices."

Here the corregidor demanded whether there
was any mark or fignature by which to afcertain
who had been the writer of thofe letters.

My lord, faid the Baron, his majefty and you
will obferve, that in this ftrange difcovery, evi-
dently made under the directing hand of Heaven,
prefumptive evidence is the utmoft we can yet
reach; the identity of the perfon murdered will
be admitted fufficiently proved, when the ring,
the armour, and the letters directed to Gonfalvo,
found with the fkeleton, the fkull of which is fplit
tranfverfely, and the inftrument lying in the place,
are taken into confideration. The queftion then
is, whether this proof be or be not fufficient to
induce your majefty to fet on foot an enquiry;

O 4

to

to call the Father Prior of the convent to account
for that crowd of fufpicious circumftances, and
thence to draw more ample proof of the guilt of
the accufed ?

This, faid the king, is certainly reafonable.

The corregidor agreed with his majefty.

Your majefty then fees, continued the Baron,
that the next confideration will be, how to do this
in fuch a manner as to prevent the cunning of
thofe concerned from rendering the enquiry abortive: and as I have turned the whole through my
mind, and have confidered it with fo much the
more attention, as I am moft concerned in the
iffue, I will, with your majefty's permiffion, fuggeft
a plan which I truft will meet with approbation.

The corregidor defired him to explain himfelf.

My fcheme, faid the Baron, is this :—In the firft
place, let fome of your lordfhip's moft intelligent
officers, duly authorifed, proceed with us to the
vaults, and there take full cognizance, and teftify
to your lordfhip in writing what fhall appear to
them: let this, along with the teftimony of the
reverend Father here, of Don Ifidor, and of Don
Alphonfo, be made up into a record, and depofited
together with the ring, armour, fabre, and letters,
in the archives of your court; on this your majefty

jefty will ground an order for the arreft of all parties fufpected; and in the execution of this, care
muft be taken to prevent any impediments, by
collufion or otherwife, being thrown in the way
of juftice. To this end, while one armed force
furrounds the caftle of Punalada on one fide, and
another the priory on the other, we, with a
chofen few of your majefty's appointment, will
enter the vault by the private paffage and be ready
to receive any one that might enter it through the
caftle. I have many reafons for expecting, from
the execution of this plan, much fuccefs, feeing
that the fudden concuffion of unexpected fear, has
often fhaken from the foul of a hardened finner, a
guilty fecret, which the deliberate operations of
juftice, nay torture itfelf, could not wring from
him.

The corregidor then declared, that notwithftanding the miraculous tenor of the whole tranfaction, every thing which had fallen from the
Baron carried fo much the fterling weight of truth,
as, joined with the evidence, and his and the
other witneffes known integrity, ferved to bear
down all doubt of his fincerity; and he entirely
approved of his plan for facilitating a full difcovery, and enfuring juftice: and in conclufion
added,

added, that he would appoint a proper perfon to go and hold the inqueft defired.

The king, on his part, affured the Baron, that on the proof of what he had advanced being eftablifhed (of which by the by he had little doubt), every practicable reparation fhould be made to him and his family : for, faid he, exclufive of the demand juftice makes on me as a fovereign, I fhall think fomething efpecially due to the friend of Alphonfo.

Alphonfo, penetrated with gratitude, knelt and kiffed the king's hand.—Long may John live the pride and glory of Caftile ! exclaimed the Baron : the reft pronounced a heart-felt amen ; and the king and corregidor retired.

Don Juan kept them all that day at his houfe, and in the evening an officer arrived with a letter from the corregidor to the Baron ; he had orders to proceed directly on the inqueft : they refolved to fet out that night ; but it was agreed that the fervants fhould remain behind, to prevent unneceffary fpeculations,

C H A P.

C H A p. XII.

IT was juft twilight when they arrived in the valley: they proceeded to the bower, where, according to a prior determination, the Baron and Don Ifidor remained with the horfes, while Father Thomas, the officer, and Alphonfo, went to the chapel. Arrived at the mouth of the fubterraneous paffage, they ftruck a light, and found the place juft as it had been left by them. The obftructions being now few, they got down without much lofs of time: Alphonfo foon found the little door that opened into the vault.—The officer entered croffing himfelf, and was fmote with horror at the fpectacle prefented to his view.—He examined the fkull—the armour—every thing—and took down an accurate account of the whole in writing. In order to eftablifh the point of the relative fituation with the convent, Father Thomas opened the cemetery, and fhewed him the bodies of the deceafed fathers of the convent, which he

likewife

likewife exactly noted, and then again returned into the vault. Alphonfo then took out the key and opened the door at which the Baron had before ftopped at the fuggeftion of the prieft.

They entered now into a long vaulted gallery, which branched off tranfverfely on either fide the door: here they ftopped to deliberate which way they fhould turn, whether to the right branch or the left. While they were in this ftate of fufpenfe, their ears were ftruck with the notes of foft mufic, which feemed to come from the extreme end of the right branch of the vaulted gallery. They paufed—the mufic died away.—Never, faid Alphonfo, did I hear fuch ravifhing founds!—They then, with as little noife as poffible, went forward:—again the mufic ftruck up, and they could diftinctly hear a female voice, as fweet as that of feraphs, accompanied by a guitar—it fung by fnatches the moft tender, melancholy notes.—They ftood and liftened attentively, but could hear no diftinct words. At the conclufion of a ftanza it ceafed, and a figh that would have rent the knotty heart of apathy itfelf, and extorted pity from the remorfelefs favage of the woods, followed it.—Alphonfo fighed refponfive.

They again as cautioufly as poffible ftept forward,

ward, and at the end of the gallery found that it again branched off to the left.—At this inftant they heard another figh, and prefently a voice, tuned by the hand of harmony itfelf, exclaimed: Oh bleffed and moft merciful redeemer! when fhall my foul take its flight, and fhelter itfelf in thy bofom from the miferies of this life?—They took advantage of the fpeaking to ftep forward without giving alarm, and perceived before them a glimmering light faintly break acrofs the gallery. Alphonfo, who carried the lamp, laid it down at the turning; and they came to a door, acrofs which near the top was cut a hole of about a foot long, and four or five inches broad, grated with fmall bars of iron. Father Thomas ftep: forward, cautioufly peeped in, and beckoned to the others to do the fame. They beheld in a low gloomy chamber, which wanted nothing but height and windows to render it magnificent, a lady on her knees before a couch praying with eyes and hands devoutly uplifted to Heaven: her face, which they could diftinctly fee, bore every mark of dignity and beauty, but faded, and ftrongly impreffed with the veftiges of care, thought, and affliction—Her lips ceafed to move— the tears gufhed in torrents from her eyes—fhe dropped her arms upon the couch, then funk down

with

with her face between her hands, uttered a heart-rending figh, and remained motionlefs. Alphonfo's foul feemed forcing its paffage through his eyes, while his heart beat fo ftrongly as to agitate his whole frame, and he breathed fhort and hard. Father Thomas feared he might be heard, and drew him away—the officer continued to obferve what paffed within. Prefently a door opened in the extreme end of the room, and he obferved a large man feemingly of above the middle time of life enter; he had a lamp in one hand, and a fword in the other—The lady ftarted, and, feeing him, arofe and fate down on the couch; he joined her, and feating himfelf with an air of familiarity by her fide, addreffed her with, Always in tears!—what, fhall I be ever patient only to excite frefh infult?—fhall I find you ftill incorrigible?—and does not the apprehenfions of my power yet fubdue your ftubborn foul?

Alas, my Lord! returned the lady, is a lapfe of fo many, many years fpent in this dreary cell under all the miferies of anxiety and incertitude—is the refolute endurance of violence, infult and opprobrious abufe—is the firmnefs with which I refifted the active endeavours of your hireling prieft, who betrayed his God, and ufed the facred privilege of confeffor to pour pernicious poifon in

my

my ear, and act the Pandar's part—is the fortitude with which I resigned my infant to that death
with which you menaced him, rather than wrong
my most beloved lord—are my vows solemnly
made and registered in Heaven—are the mortifying scorn with which I have always treated your
protestations, and my contempt and hatred of your
hideous person—are those fervent petitions which
now for many, many years I have every hour of
the undistinguished day and night wasted to Heaven with the sighs of an afflicted heart, to smite
your guilty head and level it with the dust—are
all those, I say, openly expressed and every day
avowed; yet insufficient to correct the presump-
tion of your heart, or convince you of the folly
as well as wickedness of your hopes?—Unhappy
wretch! Pity for whose weakness would counter-
vail my indignation for any crimes less than
yours—begone! — or if nothing will convince
your senseless vanity, nor quell the fiend that
works within you, but assurance sealed with blood,
take my life—But oh! that would be mercy, an
act above the reach of your gloomy soul—Nay,
strain all your cruelty to the utmost, let all the
petty vengeance of a base soul be let loose upon
me, but cease to torture me with repetition of your
foul polluted vows, nor insult the ashes of my
murdered

murdered husband, whose arm, when living; could have crushed you into dust.

Once for all then, hear me, madam, said the man.—Here I solemnly swear—

How shalt thou swear? By what?—unhappy man, who hast already broken every tie that binds man to man, every bond that connects the creature with its creator; who hast so far outstripped all precedent of sin, as to leave your crimes without a name, and run beyond the pale even of Heaven's mercy.

If then, interrupted he, if there be yet left in Heaven's mercy one ray of hope to gleam upon my soul, may it be cut off, and consign me to utter darkness if I do not now once for all speak the irrevocable purpose of my mind—my firm, unalterable resolve—Your son, as I have already told you, convicted of treacherous designs against my castle and my life, now awaits his doom in chains.

Unhappy wretch! returned the lady—think, think! nor heap new perdition on your soul—think that all is not treachery which the coward suspicion of a guilty heart proclaims so—What! was his talking with a few armed men treachery?

Nay, interrupted the man, but he mentioned a name which shews—

What

What name? exclaimed the lady exultingly—Oh, mother of mercy! perhaps it may—Oh if there were a name, the very found of which would blaft open the gates of your concealment—dart vengeance quick as the piercing lightening through your caftle—and hurl you from your blind fecurity!—Even now, fpite of yourfelf, you betray your bafe fears—and (rare union of coward-ice and rafhnefs!)while you tremble at the lion's roar indulge in cruel fport, and goad its young-one in the cage.

Hear me, proud woman! interrupted the man haftily—hear me, nor difturb me with your raving—By that oath which i've juft fworn, he dies!—One only hing, and that you know, can fave him.

Then let him die—a fon of the houfe of Rayo knows how to die, but cannot know difhonour—nor can Heaven receive a more delightful facrifice, than that of a virtuous fon immolated at the fhrine of his parent's honour.

By Heavens, he fhall die before you!

And think'ft thou, monfter, foolifh as depraved! that my foul, elevated by the dignity of virtue above the common feelings of our nature, and cheered by the all-fuftaining voice of religion, can, after yield-ing up the life of my child, ftoop to tremble at the manner of his death?—No, let it be! and draw

P

from

from it, and from your own feelings, this inftruction, that as there is no circumftance too trivial
to ftrike terror to the heart of guilt; fo there is
no calamity, however horrible to man's nature,
that the firm foul of virtue and religion cannot
look fearlefs in the face, and fuffer with a fmile.

One week, faid he rifing, I allow you for deli-
liberation: at the end of that time fhould'ft
thou remain ftubborn, though my own death
fhould go hand in hand with it, and eternal
perdition wait on death, it fhall be done!—Then
moving to the door, and cafting at her a look full
of horror and fury, he faid fternly, Think upon
it! and withdrew.

For one week then, faid the lady, I fhall not be
afflicted with the fight of you—Oh happy truce,
worthy a rich facrifice!

Remember, faid he returning, a week!—By
Heavens but a week!—and again retired.

The lady then threw herfelf down upon the
couch, wept bitterly, and remained immoveable—
The prieft then withdrew and brought away the
others, faying, it was probable that nature exhaufted was finking into fleep.

And who may thofe people be? faid the officer.
—Hufh, faid the prieft, let us begone!—They returned into the vault, and fhut the door after them.

Be

—Be particular, faid the prieft to the officer, in noting the converfation you have juft heard.

I fhall, faid the officer:—this armour we muft bear away — it is the corregidor's orders — the reft I can well report.

Every thing paffed with the fecrecy they wifhed : they found the Baron and Don Ifidor with the horfes, and mounting, were out of the valley by day-break.

As they went along, Father Thomas, in whofe mind the expiration of the week appeared with all its horrors, preffed them to haften forward, telling them in general terms, that if they were not back in a week, dreadful confeqüences might enfue—and as it was full four days journey to Burgos, at the common rate of travelling, it was found expedient to put their horfes to the pufh.

The Baron could not comprehend what Father Thomas meant, nor would the latter tell him, but amufed him with a ftory of his own fiction. The truth was, Father Thomas knowing the warm, impetuous temper of the Baron, was afraid to tell him what paffed in the vault, left it fhould roufe him to fome act of rafhnefs that might defeat all their projects, and had enjoined Alphonfo and the officer to be filent on that head.

They

They arrived at Burgos on the evening of the third day; and the urgency of the cafe being a fufficient excufe, the officer that night made a faithful report to the corregidor, and Don Juan hearing the whole went to the King.—They viewed the armour, and Don Juan having it cleaned in the proper places, faid, he would bear witnefs to its being Gonfalvo's. The prieft then gave an exact account of the fcene in the lady's chamber—The King was horror ftruck—Never, faid he, have I heard of fuch accumulated guilt— The Baron was like a perfon bereft of his fenfes—he meditated—attempted to fpeak—paufed—ftarted —fmote his breaft—caft up his eyes to Heaven— groaned aloud—The King perceived his agitation, and was much affected. It muft be, faid the Baron at laft, with difficulty getting forth his words—it muft be fhe—it is, it is my daughter! and that youth to whom we fpoke at the caftle is her fon, Fernando is her fon; then turning to the King, and bending his aged knee—Oh Sire! can thy heart, which never has known forrow but by the name, conceive the pangs of an old man, on whofe grey head it has pleafed Heaven to fhower down forrows, thick as it fends the hail upon the earth—canft thou in this moment of fufpenfe, when the cloud of his misfortunes break-

ing

ing emits one ray of light—when all his hopes hang on the flight tenure of a tyrant and a murderer's will—canft thou fympathize with him in his feelings, and with a virtuous fketch of the imagination beguile yourfelf into his condition? Here the king, much affected, endeavoured to raife him.—Yes thou canft, continued the Baron; —I fee it—heaven-born pity beams in your eyes, and through them fpeaks confolation to my heart. Oh Baron, interrupted the king, rife! Ah no, my liege! let old Rayo, who has often made the infidels and enemies of Caftile bow the knee before your grandfire's throne, here cling to the ground till his boon be granted. I grant it, faid the king, giving him his hand—Rife, Baron, I befeech you.

My boon, then, faid the Baron rifing, is, that this very night meafures may be taken to fecure the prior and heads of the convent of Vallefanto, and the Marquis of Punalada with his domeftics.

I will not only do fo, faid the king, but will even take it as a favour if Don Juan will go along with you. Don Juan cheerfully affented, and received orders to direct three troops of horfe to hold themfelves inftantly in readinefs to march. Meantime, faid the king, I fhall fend for the

arch-

archbifhop of Toledo to attend me, in order to get his warrant, without which I fhould not wifh to touch the convent.

The next morning all marched properly inftructed and authorifed; the Baron and his party going out of the city by a different route from Don Juan and the troops. On the evening of the fourth day they reached the valley, and according to the plan fettled between them, the Baron and Don Ifidor and two troops went round by the Villaverde road to the caftle, while one led by Don Juan, and attended by Father Thomas and Alphonfo, went towards the convent, where, after giving proper inftructions to the commanding officer, they left them, and proceeded to the chapel, removed the ufual impediments, and found their way into the vault. Here having viewed every thing, Alphonfo drew forth the key, opened the door, entered the tranfverfe paffage, and proceeded gently towards the door that looked into the lady's chamber. They perceived her lying afleep upon a couch, and a lamp burning on a table by her fide. Here they impatiently waited the found of the trumpet from the caftle-gate, each ftraining his eyes to get a view of the lady's face, yet daring not to make a noife. At length the wifhed-for

signal

fignal was given—the trumpet founded—an uni-verfal clamour and noife was heard at a diftance—The lady ftill flept—A clanking of chains was dif-tinguifhed approaching the chamber on the far fide; and the door flying open, the man feen before ap-peared dragging along the ground by the hair, with one hand, the unfortunate Fernando, who being fhackled could not ftand, and in the other brandifh-ing a fabre, while fury, wildnefs and terror rendered his countenance beyond expreffion horrible—Here, Madam! faid he, dragging the youth to the foot of the couch—the hour is come, and your fon is brought to die at your feet!—The lady fuddenly ftarted from her fleep, fcreeched, threw herfelf upon her fon, and fwooned.

You have now, faid he to Fernando, brought treafon to my doors, and 'tis fit that you fhould die: to make vengeance more complete, I will wait till your mother revives to behold it. Al-phonfo could no longer reftrain himfelf, but rufh-ing againft the door fplintered it to pieces.—Villain! cried he, hold your murderous hand, or this inftant thou dieft!

The Marquis ftarted at the word—and looked up. At the fight of Alphonfo the fword fell from his hand—his hair ftood erect—his knees knocked againft each other—his face affumed the very

image

image of death—he was bereft of speech with the agony of his fear, and his eyes glared without any appearance of motion——At length he threw himself proftrate on his face, and fell into a fwoon.

Meantime the lady, affifted by Don Juan, came to herfelf—and ftared wildly round her.—Is he dead? faid fhe—Oh no! Is not this he? Alas! I have not feen my child thefe many years!—She then looked down eagerly on her fon, who, on his part, feeing his friend Alphonfo, exclaimed in ecftacy—Good God! is this my Alphonfo?—Surely it is—Ah! where, Alphonfo! where is the Baron de Rayo?—Hah!—where—what faidft thou, my child? did you fay the Baron de Rayo? it cannot be—Ah, no!—my father—my beloved father is long fince numbered with the dead—elfe I fhould not be here, nor you my child.—No —my father is now in company with thofe chrif-tian heroes, whofe valour and virtues adorned human nature, finging hymns of glory to the Moft High!

While this was paffing in the fubterranean part of the caftle, the officer had fummoned, in the king's name, the lord of the caftle to open the gates.—The Marquis, who had, in his confter-nation at the firft account of their arrival, pro-

ceeded

ceeded to the act of defperation already mentioned, was fought for in vain over the caftle—Attendants ran up and down—and the Prior, perceiving the convent gate befieged by a troop, immediately betook himfelf to his wonted paffage to feek the Marquis:—his route lay through the left branch of the vaulted gallery already mentioned, and thence along by the door of the lady's chamber. Hearing a noife of words, he thought the Marquis was there, and in his precipitation burft into the chamber, juft as the lady had ended her laft fentence. Nothing could exceed his aftonifhment—he ftarted back—but fhe faw him, and breaking off fuddenly—Hah! officious pandar, faid fhe, art thou come to help thy lord and mafter, and fill up the meafure of thy iniquities by new butcheries? Father, faid Don Juan, ftepping up to him, I arreft you in the name of the king. Then turning to Alphonfo, and pointing to the Marquis, who ftill lay proftrate—Lift up that recreant lord, and let us bring them both from this place towards the caftle, which it fhould feem lies this way. They then lifted up the Marquis, who opening his eyes, ftared at Alphonfo, and bellowed out aloud—It is, it is the murdered Gonfalvo!— They hurried him and the prior fuddenly through the door by which his lordfhip had entered, while
the

the lady, who had all along kept her eyes fixed on her fon Fernando, at the name of Gonfalvo, caft up her eyes and caught a fide glimpfe of Alphonfo, juft as he pufhed the Marquis through the door. She inftantly fcreamed aloud—ftarted from the body of her fon, and calling out, My hufband! my hufband! flew towards Alphonfo—while he and Don Juan were beyond meafure fhocked and aftonifhed. Don Juan apprehending her to be delirious laid hold of her, and with fome refift-ance on her part brought her back to the couch. She fcreamed and ftruggled violently.—Oh vil-lain! villain! are you too a murderer? and will you keep me from my long loft lord whom I thought dead?—She then paufed, and turning to him faid, Is he indeed alive, or has my fight been bleffed with the fhade of my beloved? For Hea-ven's fake, dear lady, faid Don Juan, compofe yourfelf, and prepare your mind for news that will delight you; for though your hufband be -not alive, your-deliverance from the tyrant is at hand, and all will yet be well. Juft at thefe words they heard a great noife—I muft go, faid Don Juan, my prefence may be neceffary.— Good heavens! faid the lady, looking earneftly at him, is not this——Alas! my recollection is gone, and time and grief have effaced names from

my

my memory—Were you not a friend of Gonfalvo's? I was.—Your name? Don Juan de
Padilla. The fame, faid fhe.—Does my father
live? faid fhe eagerly—.He does, replied Don
Juan—I muft away and will bring him to
you foon.

Then faid fhe, I have yet a father and a child—
but I have loft my hufband! yet, bleffed be he
that hath in the general wreck of our houfe fpared
me what he hath.

Don Juan at length found his way, directed by
the noife, through a long, dark-vaulted gallery,
which led him into a fmall clofet, whence, following the found, he paffed through feveral cham-
bers, till at laft he came to a large hall, where
he found the Marquis and the Prior furrounded
by a crowd of foldiers and domeftics, to whom
the Baron was explaining the nature of the affair,
and the manner of the difcovery of the Marquis's
villainy—while he fate creft-fallen, with his head
dropped upon his breaft—and the Prior endeavoured to expoftulate with the Baron, and throw
the whole odium of the bufinefs upon the Marquis.

The entrance of Don Juan put an end to
the whole cabal—he ordering the Marquis and
Prior to be confined in feparate places, to prevent

vent any collusive arrangement with regard to their confession.

Fear not, said the Prior, I will confess all— Here I shake off all that false lenity which has hitherto restrained me from discovering this bad man's guilt: every thing that I know, from the beginning to this minute—even the little share of sin that I have had by winking so long at it, shall be candidly and without reserve laid before you.

'Here the Marquis started, like one suddenly roused from sleep——To the king's mandate, said he, addressing Don Juan, I bow with due submission, and shall attend you, Sir, whithersoever you shall be ordered to lead me : but let not the calm artifice, the monkish subtilty of that wretch, heap more guilt upon me than is properly my own. What share he has had in my misfortunes you shall all soon know. Then will you see what mischiefs may lurk beneath the monkish cowl. Heaven incensed, demands expiation of a foul offence, and shall have it—if the most unequivocal avowal and ample confession, rendering to the last letter of truth justice to him and to myself can lead to it. To this end I will draw up, and afterwards sign in presence of you all, a full confession of this dark affair.

affair. Let me have but two hours to myfelf for the purpofe, undifturbed in my clofet.

After confulting together, it was agreed that he fhould be allowed the time required, but not in his clofet. Pen, ink, and paper, were therefore allowed him in a room in a diftant wing of the caftle, where he could get at no papers or evidences to deftroy them—while guards were ftationed beneath the windows and at the door. Mean time they entered his clofet, where they locked up and fealed all his papers—They then proceeded to the vault, where the young Fernando was releafed, and the Baron once more preffed to his bofom his long-loft daughter.

When the indefcribable emotions of paternal affection and filial reverence had a little fubfided into calmnefs, they led her forth into the upper part of the caftle, where, the unaccuftomed air and light overcoming her, fhe fwooned, and was put to bed by a female attendant of the caftle; while the Baron, Don Juan and the reft continued their fearch, and were aftonifhed at the number of vaults and fubterraneous paffages which lay in all directions round the foundations of the caftle and convent. They concluded by clofing up the vault where the bones of Gonfalvo lay, till

arrange-

arrangements fhould be made for a proper in-
terment.

Three hours had been thus fpent, when they
returned to the hall, and finding that the Marquis
had not yet come forth, proceeded to the room
where he was : they knocked at the door, and re-
ceiving no anfwer, opened it, and found the unhappy man covered with blood, and in the ago-
nies of death—They raifed him up, and he expired.
He had cut the great artery of the neck entirely
a-crofs, and fo had rendered affiftance, had it
been at hand on the minute, ineffectual. A paper frefh written, and figned by him, lay on the
table. Don Juan took it up, and delivered it to
Father Thomas, who read it aloud in the following words :

CHAP.

C H A P. XIII.

THIS caftle was once a nunnery, and is coeval
with the convent of Vallefanto ; this will account
for the number of fubterraneous paffages which
unite them : in an invafion of the Moors they
took poffeffion of it, and difperfed the nuns, after
having violated their chaftity. One of my an-
ceftors drove them hence, and got the eftate from
the king as the reward of his valour : hence the
convent became in fome fort under the dominion
of the lord of this caftle, who, by various en-
trenchments on the rights of the church, got at
laft the fole appointment of prior to the convent.
The monfter who is now prior was bred by my
father's charity about this caftle, a mendicant
child ; he was the companion of my youth, the
depofitory of my fecrets—the confidant and
agent of my amours ; and when by my father's
defire he took the habit, he became my confeffor.

On

On my coming to the eftate I kept him in my family, intending to give him the priory on the death of the then incumbent. Meantime I married, and found in the Marchionefs a moft tender and affectionate companion, and a gentle corrector of my vices. I was happy:—but the enemy of mankind envied me my blifs, and in the fhape of that friar plunged me into eternal—endlefs—endlefs perdition!

Gonfalvo brought his wife to Toledo—I faw her, and was fmitten with her beauty—yet for a time I had virtue enough to refift the flame. I confeffed it to Father Pedro. Again I told—again bewailed my mifery, and lamented the flame that confumed me.—He ufed his endeavours to mitigate it, by letting in at firft a ray of finful hope.—Here I firft ftumbled—and never recovered myfelf till I fell into the abyfs of guilt in which you fee me: with the fubtle cafuiftry of a church logician, he refined away the criminality of adulterous indulgence, by oppofing it to the fin of fuicide, for fo he denominated my forbearing, at the rifk of my life and health, which were obvioufly declining. He laid a plan:—even now, after an interval of twenty years fpent in buffeting the affaults of confcience, my blood runs cold to think of it! He not only devifed the diabo-

8   lical

lical plan, but he aided in the execution of it.—
The Marchionefs was in the way—fhe fell fick—
the reverend father found her a phyfician, and fhe
died.—The prior of this convent fell fick, and
died alfo.

Hitherto all fell out, or rather was conducted
to the, accomplifhment of the chief plot—Gonfalvo was made to believe that the king looked
with an eye of luft upon his wife, and intended
to ravifh her from him : I was his clofe counfel-
lor and friend, and perfuaded him to carry her
away with the utmoft fecrecy, and depofit her
in a nunnery, which I told him was here. The
Father was their guide—I haftened to the caftle,
while he conducted them to the convent, and by
a private door let them through the convent into
the cemetery, from which, he faid, the lady fhould
pafs into the nunnery. She was accordingly led
into a remote room of this caftle near the paffage
to the cemetery, while I went forward with two
affaffins, hired for the purpofe by the prieft.—
We led Gonfalvo into that vault where his body
was found, and as he ftooped to enter (his great
height making him ftoop more than us, and he
confequently being more expofed), one of the affaffins fmote him with a fabre, and fplit his fkull.
—With the prieft's help we took a fhell and fome

boards from the cemetery, and putting him in buried him on the fpot. When this was done, the prieft whifpered me privately, that our fafety demanded the death of the aſſaſſins. He did not allow me time to deliberate, but turning fuddenly round plunged a dagger into the breaſt of him that was neareſt, and then aſſaulting the other, who refifted, I difpatched him with my fword on the inſtant.

The virtue of the lady fet her above all my efforts. The officious churchman propofed force. —I attempted it, but in vain—the feeble efforts of a weak woman were fufficient to beat me from that objeɛt, for the attainment of which I had waded through a fea of blood.

By bribing the nurfe I got her child into my hands—Fernando is he—I daily threatened him with death if ſhe did not comply. In vain—ſhe refifted—and remains as pure in perfon as in foul.

By a feigned tale to the King I got all the family eftates confifcated, and put in my poffeffion. If my crimes admit of any mitigation, let it not be forgot that I faved Baron de Rayo from Peter's fury; who, incenfed with the Baron's haughtinefs, would, but for me, have put him to death.—Let this fpeak in favour of my inno-

L   cent

cent daughter.—Fernando's nurſe lives—ſhe is
in——

PUNALADA.

Here the knocking at the door cut off the reſt,
and left them in doubt about the nurſe.

Don Juan ordered the domeſtics, who were at
hand, to take the body of the Marquis—then
ſealed the papers in preſence of all, and gave ſtrict
orders to keep the Prior in cuſtody. He then
took Fernando, who was ſo bewildered with the
wonders of the day that he ſcarcely knew whether
what paſſed was reality or a dream, by the hand,
and ſaluted him by the name of Gonſalvo, congratulating him at the ſame time on the fortunate diſcovery of his parents, and his certain ac-
ceſſion to rank and fortune. The Baron, little
leſs bewildered, looked at Fernando, and ever and
anon graſped his hand with a tenderneſs mixed
ſometimes with aſtoniſhment, and ſometimes with
doubt.

While they were making the proper arrangements for ſecuring every thing to abide the King's
pleaſure, a woman came in and informed them
that the lady had recovered from the fit, but was
delirious. The Baron and Fernando immediately
proceeded to her chamber—Come hither, my

Q 2

father,

father, faid fhe, and give your daughter a laſt bleſſing—and you, my ſon, to Fernando, come and take mine.

Why? my child, faid the Baron, kneeling down by her—why a laſt bleſſing? This ſickneſs, produced by the ſhocks and furpriſes of the day, and the change of air, will ſoon wear off, and days of happineſs will yet attend you. Never, my father—oh never! I have ſeen that which aſſures me—What have you ſeen, my Maria? Oh my moſt beloved and moſt refpeéted ſire! think not that from any delirium of the mind, any temporary weakneſs of intelleét, proceeds what I am to tell you—it is, it is true—As I do live, I ſaw my Henry, my huſband! In that hideous vault I this day ſaw him—ſo lovely—ſo graceful—ſo majeſtic, as when firſt you bleſſed me with the words, "Gonſalvo ſhould be mine." Calm, my dear, faid the Baron tenderly—calm thoſe violent agitations, which proceed from error, an error which I can explain, and will effeétually. He whoſe figure has ſo deceived you, is the ſon of Don Iſidor de Haro, your couſin and Gonſalvo's, but ſo exaétly the counterpart of my ſon, that I never ſee him with-out aſtoniſhment! His likeneſs ſtruck the guilty Marquis into a paroxyſm of horror that ſhook rea-ſon from its ſeat, and made him his own accuſer.

Iſidor

Ifidor lives, then ? said fhe. He does, replied the Baron; the friend, the fupport, and the protection of your father's age ; and to this fon of his we owe, under God, the difcovery of this horrid affair. As foon as reft has fitted you for a new furprife, you fhall fee them both, and hear every thing : meantime, my child, let this affurance appeafe the perturbation of your mind, and try and take fome reft. You are now fafe, continued he, refcued from the ravifher and murderer's hands ; reftored to light, to life, to family and friends—bend in gratitude to that God, who, by a fignal and miraculous interpofition, hath brought about your deliverance.

These words drew tears from her eyes—fhe funk in grateful humility into her bed—took her father's hand and kiffed it—then her fon's— and, turning without faying a word, left them to depart.

Meantime an account of the Marquis's death and the arreft of the Prior reached the convent— all there was uproar—the guard would let no one pafs.—At length a requifition was fent from the young lady there, to be permitted to pafs to the caftle and fee her father, though dead—This was readily granted. She flew round—paffed through the court-yard, and entered the great hall in

a ftate.

a ſtate of diſtraction, calling aloud on her father—
She paſſed by Don Iſidor, Don Juan, and every
one who met her, without ſeeming conſcious of
their preſence—At length ſhe met Alphonſo—at
ſight of him ſhe ſtopped ſhort, and ſtared with a
fixed attention;—her boſom heaved—her colour
ſhifted from red to white, and back again ;—her
limbs trembled, and ſhe was falling when he,
caught her in his arms.—She remained inſenſible
for ſome time—at length recovering, ſhe again
regarded him with a ſteady gaze, and in a deep
piercing tone ſaid, Then thou art he, and the prediction is accompliſhed—the houſe of Puṇalada is
in ruins !—Then breaking from him, Shew me,
ſhew me, ſaid ſhe, where my father is ! and darted
from their ſight,

That day Don Juan and Alphonſo, with one
troop of horſe, and the Prior their priſoner, ſet out
for Burgos, as well to lay the whole before the
King, as procure a proper conveyance to remove
the lady from the caſtle. The King was horror-
ſtruck and aſtoniſhed—he forthwith called a coun-
cil, of which the Archbiſhop of Toledo made
part, in which it was determined that the Prior
ſhould be handed over to the grand inquiſitor—
that the attainder of Gonſalvo ſhould be entirely
eraſed from the records of the court—that the
title

title of Punalada should be extinguished, and the
Marquis's whole fortunes confiscated—and that so
much of them as had before belonged to the Baron
and Gonsalvo, together with one half of his own
original estate, reserving a small annuity for his
daughter, should pass over to the Baron and his
issue—the King reserving the other half to himself, to bestow on Alphonso. That day proclama-
tion was made of the Marquis's death, attainder
and forfeiture, and of the reinvestiture of the Baron, with his estate, rank, and title.

They returned to the castle of Punalada, with a
carriage of the King's to convey the lady to
court, the King being desirous of offering her
every mark of distinction, and a vehicle for the
remains of Gonsalvo... When they arrived
they found that Don Rodrigo had been there,
and, on being refused admission to his uncle's
closet, and possession of the castle, had set off in a
rage, threatening them all with the indignation of
the King—that the Marquis's body had been
consigned to the earth with the ignominy attached
to suicide—and that the lady was recruited, and
not only willing, but desirous to quit the castle.

When Alphonso was, after proper precaution,
introduced to her, her astonishment was greater
than ever it was before—She knew not what to

think

think—what to fay—or how to conduct herfelf—
She looked at every one round her in turn, to read
in their faces fome folution of a myftery that fhe
could not help thinking was involved in it—Her
hufband, her beloved Gonfalvo ftood before her—
Aftonifhment drank up her tears—fhe could not
cry—yet fhe would if fhe could, to eafe her heart.
With much difficulty at length fhe faltered out,
Is this then, really, the fon of Don Ifidor de
Haro? and is Fernando mine, or is it done to
mock me?—The Baron looked grave—Don Ifidor more fo—It is fo, faid fhe—yet it's ftrange. It
is the will of God, faid the Baron, and fhall we
finfully prefume to fcan it? No, faid fhe, no, however irreconcileable it may be to our weak fenfes,
it muft be right—Here fhe paufed. This confufion of refemblance, faid fhe, Don Ifidor, points
out that union which fhould always fubfift between
our children; therefore fuffer me to treat Alphonfo, and this our fon, as equally our children.
You fpeak my very foul, madam, faid Don Ifidor,
for my attachment to your fon is not lefs than
yours to mine; and there feems already to fubfift
between them the affection of brothers. The
youths were delighted—all parties were as happy
as their different circumftances may be fuppofed
to admit of. Preparations were made for
their

their departure—The Baron got the remains of Gonſalvo, even to the duſt in the cheſt, carefully put into a coffin, and laid in the vehicle, Then after ſeeing the King's officers take poſſeſſion and ſeal down every thing, the Baron, Father Thomas and Don Iſidor got with the lady into the carriage and proceeded towards Burgos, while Alphonſo and his friend Fernando rode by their ſide.

CHAP.

C H A P. XIV.

IT was pretty far advanced in the night of the fourth day before they came near the city : Alphonfo and Fernando, taken up with reflection and mutual congratulations on their happinefs, dropped behind, and had fallen into converfation on the beauty of the night and the brightnefs of the moon, when, juft as the carriage turned the corner at the extreme end of an olivary, and got out of hearing, a band of armed ruffians rufhed from the covert of the trees upon the two youths, who had no perfon to aid them in refiftance but Pierrot. Before they were prepared to defend themfelves, one of the ruffians from behind buried a dagger in the fhoulder of Alphonfo, and felled him to the earth. Fernando on the inftant faw the ftroke given, and fmote the ruffian to the ground ; he then vigoroufly attacked the reft, and Pierrot coming up to his aid beat them off all but three, who lay weltering under the wounds given them by Fernando. Pierrot then purfued and ftopt the coach, relating at the fame time what had paffed—

Don

Don Alphonfo, faid he, is killed, and we may all at once put an end to ourfelves. The lady fcreamed —Don Ifidor burft from the carriage, and, followed by the Baron, ran up to the field of action, and found Fernando weeping over the body of Alphonfo:—Alas, my brother, my brother, my friend! but one inftant fooner and I fhould have faved you—Oh! would to Heaven the dagger had met my heart inftead of yours: but, unhappy that I am, I faw the blow but time enough to revenge, and fave my own worthlefs life, while thine is loft. Where, faid Don Ifidor, where is my boy?—where is my Alphonfo?—Let us lift him up, faid the Baron; perhaps life my yet be in him. Gallop forward, faid Father Thomas to Pierrot, and fee if there be a houfe at hand, to which we can carry him; and go you and bring a furgeon directly —perhaps fomething may yet be done. Juft at this inftant, a patrole of the Ronda * came up mounted. The Baron hailed them—Here hath been murder committed, faid he; have you got a light? —Yes, faid the officer, and difplaying a dark lantern difmounted and examined thofe on the ground. Alphonfo was bleeding profufely; they lifted him up, tore off his coat, and perceived that

* A patrole or watch in Spain.

the

the wound had entered his shoulder-blade very deep : they did their utmost to stop the effusion of blood, and the captain of the troop being informed by one of his people, that the carriage in waiting belonged to the King, drew forth a leathern bottle with wine, and poured some of it down Alphonso's throat—He soon exhibited some slight tokens of life, his pulse moved. They brought him to the carriage, where they found Donna Maria inconsolable ; and by the direction of the officer moved forward to an inn not far distant, while he and his men took charge of the wounded ruffians, and brought them after.

Alphonso was laid on a bed at the inn with little symptom of life—a surgeon soon attended, and declared that it was impossible he could recover. Donna Maria was distracted, and, impelled by an unaccountable feeling which overcame form, hung upon him and kissed his clay-cold lips. She was at last drawn away to give room to the surgeon, who, examining narrowly, began to be of opinion that the wound had not reached any vital part, and observed that he must have been hurt elsewhere : he therefore examined him carefully, particularly about the head, and found a considerable swelling just above the ear— Here, said he, is the chief injury ; can you tell how

he

he received it, or from what fort of weapon? He
got but one ftroke, replied Fernando, and that
was in the fhoulder. Then the hurt in the head
has procceded from his weight in falling, and the
lofs of blood from the fhoulder is in that cafe
rather ufeful than injurious. While they were
thus fpeaking, Alphonfo began to breathe hard,
then groaned : the furgeon ordered a glafs of water, with which he wetted his lips, letting a little
down—Still the word was death.

Meantime the officers of the Ronda had got the
wounded affaffins to the inn. One appeared, from
his equipments, to be a gentleman of confiderable
rank, but he was in as hopelefs a ftate as Alphonfo: another was in the livery of a fervant; and a
third had the appearance of a bravo. The two
laft were coming to themfelves, but the firft
feemed quite fenfelefs though he breathed; they
were all defperately wounded, particularly the
gentleman, whofe arm was cloven at the joint of
the fhoulder almoft from his body.

As the accident happened at the diftance of lefs
than a league from the city of Burgos, Don Ifidor,
on his arrival at the inn, wrote off to Don Juan,
informing him of the affair, and intreating proper
affiftance to be fent out. Don Juan himfelf arrived
in two hours after the meffenger was difpatched,

and

and the King's surgeon along with him, who, on examining Alphonso, enquired whether he had indicated any disposition to vomit? and on being answered in the negative declared it to be his opinion, that he had only been extremely stunned with the fall, and added, that in all probability he would soon come to himself. He ordered his head to be chafed with warm spirits, his extremities to be rubbed, and some warm wine poured down his throat: in short, he took his measures so well, that before morning the youth was restored to his senses, though extremely weak. Don Juan did every thing he could to cheer the Baron and Don Isidor, assuring them that the King intended to make ample amends to the family for the injuries it had sustained; and that he intended the first honours in the state for Alphonso, whom he loved more than any of his favourites, though much had been done to injure him in his opinion: —nay such, he said, was the attachment of the King, that he would not inform him of the present accident before he came away, to avoid giving him unnecessary pain.

When the two inferior assassins came to themselves, Don Juan, the Baron, and Don Isidor were informed of it, and coming to the room where they were, Don Juan was immediately described

scried by him who wore the livery. Whose servant are you? said Don Juan severely. I am
the servant of Don Rodrigo de Calvados, said the
fellow. Oho! said Don Juan—and where is your
master? There, your honour, said the fellow,
pointing significantly to a bench where the gentleman's body lay.—Then it was he who set you on
this enterprise? said Don Juan. God bless your
honour, returned the fellow, I knew not what I
was going about till I was in the very heart of it:
this honest man here, who, God bless us! looks
liker the devil than a man, will tell you more—
I was only a servant. Don Juan looking at the
fellow perceived that he was a bravo, and ordered
the two to be immediately carried under a strong
guard to jail.

The next day Alphonso was much recovered,
but complained of a violent pain from the wound
in his shoulder: he was however declared by the
surgeon to be able to proceed slowly in the carriage to Burgos. The gentleman assassin, Don
Rodrigo too, was able to proceed on a litter; a
strong guard was ordered for him, and he was de-
posited in the jail, and a surgeon ordered to attend him: his mother was almost mad with vexa-
tion and disappointment—but all her interest, all
her tears, all her falsehoods, and all her address
were

were of no avail; she could get no one hardy enough to apply to the King in his favour.

During Alphonso's illness Donna Maria never quitted him, but when delicacy required.

But, a considerable time having elapsed, and the wound continuing in the same state, the surgeon expressed his surprise at the slowness of the process, and frequently animadverted on symptoms of a feverish kind, for which he could not account. One day making those remarks in the hearing of Pierrot, that honest soul said, that he fancied he could tell the cause of it.

Why, what is the cause of it, wiseman? said Don Isidor.—Love, your honour, replied Pierrot, bluntly. Love!—in the name of God, with whom? I am sure, your honour, I don't know—and I believe it is more than he knows himself: the picture that hangs about his neck, perhaps, may tell—though I doubt that too, for they were strangers.

Are you mad, fellow? said the Baron hastily. No, your worship, replied Pierrot, I am not, I hope; I do the best at least that I can to avoid it: for I neither go out to seek fighting adventures, nor do I fall in love with every pretty girl in distress, which seems to me to be the ways of going mad now-a-days—I will tell you what I know. He

7   then

then told him of the adventure with the two
ladies in Portugal—concluding with an affurance,
that fince his young mafter had feen them, he
never had had one hour's peace, nor, he believed,
been right in his head.

Don Ifidor feemed extremely uneafy—retired to
a room—wrote letters, and difpatched a meffenger with them inftantly down to the caftle of
Duero. The reft of the day he feemed extremely
unhappy, nor could the Baron or any of his
friends account for the ftrange alteration in his
manner.

Next day he put the queftion of his love with
fome delicacy to Alphonfo; who candidly acknow-
ledged, that a lady he had met with on his travels
in Portugal had gained entire poffeffion of his
affections—and though he fcarcely hoped ever to
fee her again, he could not help cherifhing the
love with which fhe infpired him, and indulging
fome fmall hopes.—He then told his father the
whole ftory, and concluded with fhewing him the
picture. At fight of the picture Don Ifidor turned pale, his lips quivered, his whole frame
trembled with the agitation of his mind—He was
for fome minutes fpeechlefs—At length breaking
filence : It is as I feared, faid he !—Oh unhappy
youth !—Good God, my father ! exclaimed Alphonfo, to what ftrange ftory is this dreadful agi-

R   tation

tation a prelude ?—Alas! my unhappy child, said
Don Ifidor, prepare to hear that which muft pierce
your foul with horror!—Yet you muft know it;
though inftant death attended the information,
you muft know it—Better to die than live one hour
in the conception of a deadly fin!—That young
lady—Good God! do I live to tell it to my fon!
—that young lady, with whom you were fo deeply
enamoured, is—your fifter!—My fifter?——Yes,
your fifter! and fhe, that lady whom you refcued
along with her; is mine—the Marchionefs Deloro.
—Then I am undone! exclaimed Alphonfo;—undone here—and loft to all eternity!

Say not fo, my child, faid Don Ifidor—we are
to believe that the Almighty, who is merciful,
will judge by the intention, and not affign the punifhment of a deliberate crime to a paffion invo-
luntary and unintentional. This horror that you
feel is in itfelf an expiation, if it be followed up
with a firm determination to expel the poifon
from your foul.

Ah, there, there, my father, there lies the horror!—I fear I muft ceafe to live ere I ceafe to
fin—if loving——

Hah! interrupted Don Ifidor—hold your im-
pious tongue, nor utter in my prefence language
fo deteftable—If fo loft in guilt as to dare the
thunder

thunder of the Almighty, which flow to execute emboldens finners—doft thou not fear that a father's indignation fhould rife and crufh you into ruin.

Alas, my father! how do you miftake me, faid Alphonfo. Perhaps I do, haftily interrupted Don Ifidor: yet it is to me a fubject of that nature, the bare imagination of which harrows up my foul:—I am not fit to fpeak upon it—I fhall therefore retire and content myfelf with offering up my prayers to Heaven in your behalf; nor will I again behold you till I have firm affurance that you have banifhed the hellifh paffion, even to the laft fhadow, from your breaft, or that death has fnatched you from its power. So faying, Don Ifidor withdrew, leaving the unhappy Alphonfo in a ftate of diftraction, horror, and grief. It was the firft time in his life that a word engendered in anger had fallen from his father—and his laft expreffions fmote him the more poignantly to the heart.

On Don Ifidor's meeting the Baron and Father Thomas, they were aftonifhed at the ftrange difcompofure of his air and countenance—they were both alarmed, and almoft in a breath afked him for Alphonfo. Would to God! faid Don Ifidor, that the

R 2   affaffin's

affaffin's poignard had cut him off ere he fhould have lived to tell the horrid tale—he is in love with his fifter ! They ftared aghaft—Yes, faid he, after telling them the ftory, it is not guilt alone that meets the fcourge in this life; for I am curfed as Punalada was, and inceftuous love blights my family !——

Hold, hold, Don Ifidor ! interrupted the prieft ; judgment belongs to God—refignation is the duty of man ; beware, therefore, that while you de-nounce vengeance againft your fon, and call him finner, you are not yourfelf dipping deeper in fin than he. It appears from your own account, that at the time he firft conceived this unhappy paffion, he knew not the objeć of it was his fifter ; in the outfet, therefore, no fin is imputable, fince we muft believe that God judges us by our means of knowledge ; to expeć him then on the inftant to diflodge a deep-rooted paffion, is to expeć more than human nature is capable of per-forming. It muft be the work of time, and ftrong virtuous refolution ;—and believe me, that every effort of his to overcome it will be more acceptable in the eyes of the Almighty, than ten thou-fand aćs of mere paffive, negative virtue. I know and will anfwer for his principles, and have no

fear

fear of the event but what arifes from the ftate of his health. I fhall therefore go and converfe with him; and, I entreat, that in the mean time you will on your part recollect, that gufts of rage and boifterous invective are above all things incompatible with the mild fpirit of that glorious religion which we all adore; though fome of us, to be judged from our actions, would feem to be ignorant of it.

CHAP.

C H A P. XV.

IN a fhort time Father Thomas returned with a face unufually imprinted with forrow: he defired that a phyfician fhould be immediately fent for, for that Alphonfo was raving mad—that he fometimes talked of his fifter, fometimes of his aunt, and fometimes called upon his cruel, cruel father.

A meffenger was direétly fent for a phyfician; he came, and declared Alphonfo to be in fuch a ftate as left little room for hope—exhaufted as he had been already, he was afraid to bleed him, and expreffed a fear that the feverifh delirium would fink upon the fpirits and carry him off. He ordered him a medicine, and, defiring to be called upon the appearance of any new fymptom, went away.

As night advanced, Alphonfo grew more outrageous, and they were broke in upon at fupper by the faithful Pierrot, who told them, that he was

tearing

tearing off the dreffings from his wounds, and
that four of them were unable to hold him.
They all directly rofe and went to his chamber;
Donna Maria herfelf would not ftay behind—
there they found him in the moft dreadful ftate
of furious infanity, tearing himfelf to pieces,
while the blood gufhed afrefh from his half-healed
wounds; and the attendants were lying about the
room, bruifed by the flings he had given them
againft the walls. The Baron directly ran to him,
pinioned his arms behind his back, and with the
wrifts of a giant held him down. Don Ifidor
came in to his affiftance, and they brought him
to fome order: when in a few minutes growing
infenfibly weak, he languifhed away, wept, and
funk into a fwoon. By this time the furgeon
who was fent for came, and prepared to re-drefs
the wound; all the patient's back was covered
with blood, and he ordered it to be wafhed while
he prepared his dreffings—Donna Maria herfelf
undertook the tafk—fhe wafhed away the blood,
while the Baron held the bafon. At length,
to the aftonifhment of all, fhe fcreamed out
—Mother of God, my fon! and funk back upon
the bed.

Does it pleafe Heaven, faid Don Ifidor, to
mock our miferies, and fend infanity throughout

R 4

us all ?—Do I dream, or has this lady dreamed ?—
Can'ft thou tell me, Baron, whither tends all this
ftrange extravagant incident that marks our fortune of late, and makes the adventures of our
houfe more like romance than reality ?

In our affairs, replied the Baron, the real is fo
interwoven with the marvellous, that the whole
feems tinged with the colours of romance, and
feeks the aid of proof: fuch proof is now before us.
This youth is her fon, and my grandfon—There
lies proof indelibly written by the hand of nature
on his body. By Heavens ! exclaimed Don Ifidor, the madnefs grows round, and I myfelf I fear
fhall fhortly catch it. If madnefs be, returned the
Baron warmly, it is with yourfelf Don Ifidor !
who hold up your own rafh opinion, founded
upon circumftances fubject to error and impofi-
tion, againft the teftimony of nature itfelf, and
boldly confront the written characters of providence—Look, fee thofe grapes painted by the hand
of nature in his mother's womb. Juft at this time
the lady, who had been fupported by Father Thomas, came to herfelf—Give me, give me my child,
faid fhe—Oh fpare him, Heaven !—Then looking
—Yes ! there, there they are—Oh my Gonfalvo !
furely fomething prophetic wrought within thy
mind on that day, when in fportive innocence you
dropped

dropped a bunch of grapes down my back—I started, softly complained being then pregnant—You then, my love, said, in playful fondness said, that if we lost our child, that would be a mark by which to know him—Alas, my love! little didst thou think by what sad calamities we should lose him, or in what horrible way he should be found—found but to be lost again for ever !

If I live, said the Baron, some strange fraud has been practised on us both—a fraud most likely never to be developed. That Gonsalvo's son has exactly this mark I can give testimony; now let us see whether Fernando has it. Fernando declared that he had not. Then it is certain, said the Baron, that this is the son of Gonsalvo.

It is strange, said Don Isidor, it is beyond all comprehension strange, that a child nursed under the inspection of—But what do I say ? To-morrow I will send off to Talavera, and have the old woman at whose place he was nursed brought, with her whole family, here.

Reserve your arguments, said Father Thomas to a fitter occasion; at present let us look to the lady, who seems to stand in need of care little less than the young gentleman.

The next morning Pierrot was dispatched to the village near Talavera, to bring the old wo-

5

man

man who had been nurfe to Don Ifidor's lady, her whole family, and the nurfe who was employed to fuckle their child, directly to Burgos, but with ftrict injunctions not to apprize them of a fentence that had paffed. During this juncture Alphonfo's fever had a fortunate crifis ; he recovered the ufe of his fenfes, and, though extremely weak, gave fome hopes of recovery. It was thought advifeable, however, to keep the difcovery a fecret from him, till fuch proof fhould be had as would put it paft a doubt one way or other.

At length Pierrot returned, and with him the nurfe who had fuckled Don Ifidor's child, and her hufband; the old woman having been fome time dead. Don Ifidor ordered them to be conducted into the room where Donna Maria was; and where the Baron, Father Thomas, and Fernando attended—it was agreed that Father Thomas fhould fpeak to her. Nurfe, faid he, I prefume you are well enough acquainted with the principles of our holy religion, and the extent to which they reach, to know the dreadful punifhment attending any kind of fraud. If you do not, I will tell you that however it may be hid from mortal eyes, it cannot be concealed from the Almighty, who will not fail to punifh it with everlafting torments : when detected here, it meets the heavieft

punifhment

punishment of the law. Of both these, nurse, you and your husband stand in imminent danger; nor can any thing but a fair confession save you from being handed over instantly to the cognizance of criminal law. Answer me, then, as you hope for mercy here, or salvation hereafter—Where is the child of Don Isidor de Haro, which you, for purposes best known to yourselves, have changed, imposing for so many years upon him the charge of a child not his own—while on the other hand you may have devoted his to misery, want, or even death?—Speak, speak the truth, and believe me nothing else can save you; for, of one part of the charge against you we have unquestionable evidence.

I will, Father! I will! exclaimed the nurse, throwing herself on her knees—I will tell the truth, and though to save myself from ruin I was guilty of concealing the story from Don Isidor, I am as innocent as the child unborn of the changing, as you shall know.

One day after I had brought Don Isidor's child home to nurse, a woman with a child on her breast called in towards the close of the day; said she was a traveller and begged a lodging— She added, that she was travelling from Andalusia to Saragossa, and must be away by break of day

next

next morning—As we never refufed a chriftian
fhelter, we defired her to ftay, and gave her fhare
of what we had. The weather was extremely hot, and we all lay out on mats in the piazza
of our cottage. Juft at day-break we heard the
ftranger move—fhe got up, and bid us adieu and
went away. We wifhed her to ftay for breakfaft ;
but fhe refufed, alledging that fhe had a long
journey before her, and muft not delay.

When we arofe, the child was afleep in the
cradle; fo that altogether the woman had been
gone three hours before I went to take it up.
Guefs my forrow and furprife, when I found
that the vile wretch had changed the child. I
knew it directly by a bunch of purple grapes on
the back, though in other refpects the children
were very like each other.

Why did you not tell Don Ifidor then? faid
the Prieft.

Had I been inclined to do fo, replied the woman, it would have been impoffible, for he and
his lady, we were told, had gone into France ; but
you fhall hear. I ran, continued fhe, directly to my
hufband, who was at work, and told him. He was
going to kill me with his fickle : he immediately
broke off from work, and went in purfuit of her,
charging me to fay nothing till his return, as he

was

was pretty fure of overtaking her. But, God help us, he was all the time going farther from her; for we afterwards found that she had told us wrong, and was going towards Andalusia, instead of turning from it. At night he returned weary and broken hearted—we knew not what to do— we feared to difcover the matter—and thought it beft to leave it to chance. The thing paft over—the old woman my lady's nurfe was deceived—and finding that we had no reafon to fear a difcovery, we thought it beft, as it could not be remedied, to fay nothing. This I call God and our Redeemer to witnefs is the whole truth, and I hope you will think that I am not fo much to be blamed.

Juft as they had done examining the woman, a letter came directed to the Baron; it was from the King's officer at Punalada caftle, and was in thefe words :

" Moft excellent Lord,

" In our fearches through the many fubterranean vaults under this caftle we found, ftarved almoft to death, a woman who fays fhe has been confined many years by the Marquis, fhe imagined at leaft fifty; but that, from her ftory otherwife, is impoffible. She adds, that fhe has a fecret of the

utmoft

utmoft confequence to unfold—briefly to this
effect:—She was the nurfe of Don Henrico Gonfalvo's fon—was feduced by a prieft (whom I
fuppofe to be the Prior) to give up the child to
the Marquis; that at laft being prevailed upon, fhe
travelled with it towards Andalufia, and falling
by accident into a cottage where a child of Don
Ifidor de Haro (whom fhe knew to be the coufin
of Gonfalvo) was at nurfe, fhe determined to
fave the child, whom fhe loved, from the intentions
of the Marquis, which fhe thought might poffibly
be wicked; and accordingly left Don Gonfalvo's
in the bed, and carried away Don Ifidor's. So
that by this account, the youth Fernando, it is
probable, is Don Ifidor's, and the other your grandchild. The woman is in cuftody, fo take your meafures accordingly.

P. S. The woman is dying, and has made oath
to this effect.

Here, faid the Baron, giving the letter to Don
Ifidor, all is cleared up—Fernando is yours—
Alphonfo is mine.
Alphonfo fhall ftill be mine, replied Don Ifidor,
for he fhall be married to my daughter—I wrote to
my fifter, who arrived at Duero caftle the day after

we

we left it, from Portugal, whence she was obliged
to fly to escape the importunities and power of an
old nobleman who had fallen in love with my
daughter. She wrote me an account of her res-
cue by a young Spaniard, long since, from Seville. I have now received her answer to my
letter; and am happy to find that the impression
Alphonso made upon her niece keeps pace with
his love for her. When Pierrot first hinted the
affair, I suspected the fact just as it turned out.
Come, Baron, said Don Isidor, let us give a loose
to joy—each of us has gained without the other
being a loser—and these events, which at first appeared so adverse, will serve to unite our families by additional bonds of affection.

The body of Gonsalvo was buried in great
pomp at Montalto; and, soon after, Alphonso received Don Isidor's daughter to his arms—was
invested with half the estates of the Marquis by
the King; the other half, with Punalada castle,
being by his desire settled on Fernando, who
inherited also his grandfather Guzman's estate.
Don Rodrigo was sent to the mines—his mother
was condemned to banishment—while the Prior
of the convent of Vallesanto was doomed to per-
petual imprisonment in the Inquisition. Father
Thomas received the priory as a gift from the
hands

hands of the Archbifhop of Seville. Laftly, the Baron lived not only to fee Alphonfo and Fernando the firft warriors in Spain, and created barons, but even to inftruct a great-grandfon in the rudiments of the fcience of warfare; and at laft died, at an amazing age, furrounded by a numerous race of heroes, the defcendants of the old and illuftrious House of Rayo.

F I N I S.